EXERCISE IN LOVE

A CONTEMPORARY ROMANCE

J THOMPSON

❁ Created with Vellum

Carly was fed up with life, it had been 5 years since she lost her family and she had dealt with it in the only way she knew how-food. Overweight, single and with a dead end job she hated, her only light in the darkness was her best friend Robyn. A forced night out for her birthday makes Carly see the world she's been missing but also brings with it a realization that she can't continue on the same path. Finding the strength inside she takes that first step to change.

Andy had been plodding along burying himself in his work, until Carly erupts into his life bringing back his love for his job and making him see what has been missing from his own life. Charmed instantly by her determined attitude, innocent spirit and hypnotised by her stunning green eyes he agrees to take her on and help her on her journey not realising shes helping him on his own at the same time.

Can Carly get over her own insecurities and accept love or will her old demons win

CHAPTER ONE

THE PAST

Carly watched the surgeon's mouth move, but her ears were just filled with white noise. He gave her a final glance filled with pity before leaving the room, the door to the waiting room closing quietly, sealing her in on her own. She bowed her head and let the sobs come. She had been left alone to deal with what no 20 year old should ever have to deal with. No kind words, no asking if she needed anyone. Just left alone.

Carly had no one left now, her family wiped out in a cruel twist of fate. Earlier that day, her parents and her older brother had been travelling into town. They only lived about a mile away from Newcastle, Stoke on Trent, but her dad had insisted on taking his car. A man driving a white van had veered into them, smashing them into the central reservation and obliterated the Vauxhall Astra that had been her dad's pride and joy. Her dad and big brother, who had been seated in the front, had died instantly after being crushed. Carly hiccupped as the sobs continued. The surgeon had told her they would have felt no pain and would have passed quickly, but she didn't know how to process that information. They had still died, the fact they went quickly didn't give her any relief from the pain that currently coursed through her body.

Carly not only felt like her heart was being ripped from her chest, but anger at the man that had taken so much from her now filtered through her veins. Of course, he had been removed from the scene with only bruises and a broken leg. How was that fair? This was all his fault, if he hadn't been so focused on his sodding mobile phone then her family would still be here. Surely no text is worth three people's lives.

Carly couldn't hold back the scream of anguish that erupted from her mouth as she fell to the floor, her knees hitting the tiles hard as she wrapped her arms around her middle and rocked. She had no one left; she was now an orphan, as the tactless surgeon had informed her.

Her mother had survived the crash, but she had to be cut out of the car by the fire service. Only then did they realise that she was in bad shape and had to be rushed to hospital and straight into emergency surgery. That was when Carly had been called, been told her family was on the brink of extinction. She had no idea how she had managed to get to the hospital so fast, couldn't remember the route she had taken or even what speed she had done. All she could remember was the intense and overwhelming need to get to the hospital as fast as she could. But it didn't change the outcome.

Her mother, the one constant and strong warrior in her life was gone. Her body unable to deal with the multitude of injuries had given up, she had died on the operating table only an hour after her brother and dad had died. The sobs continued, each one jerking

Carly's body with their power. The grief too much for Carly to take, she curled up on the cold floor and continued to cry.

She became lost in the memories of her last moments with her family, desperately needing to feel the love and comfort she had from having them in her life.

"Carly babes, drive safe to work ok? You know what those idiots are like on the road."

Carly rolled her eyes but smiled, this was the same lecture she got every morning before work.

"I will Mum, I promise."

"Good, now come and give me a love." Carly's mum held her arms open wide and waited for Carly to step into them, engulfing her in a hug full of love and warmth, the smell of Chanel no 5 filled her nose and she breathed it in. Her mum loved the simple things in life but her love for that perfume knew no bounds, regardless of how expensive it was.

"Have a fab day my little Carly bug, don't work too hard. I love you."

Carly kissed her mum on the cheek "I love you too Mum, have fun today"

Carly chuckled at her mum as she pulled a face. "Ha! Fun, is that what you call it? Sitting around waiting for your brother to finish his aptitude test. We are going to be bored out of our minds."

There was no anger to her words as she placed a mug of coffee in front of Carly's dad.

"Don't worry spud, I will keep your mum occupied, just keep those fingers crossed your brother doesn't balls things up this time."

Carly snorted with laughter as her brother looked up from the table having ploughed through his bacon and eggs.

"What? I won't mess it up Dad, I just got confused last time."

Carly laughed as her dad pulled his 'are you serious face' before she kissed his cheek and walked around the table to her big brother. Regardless of the five year age gap, they were close and she loved her over protective brother to the moon and back.

Wrapping her arms around his neck, she kissed his cheek.

"You've got this bro, go show them who's boss."

"You got it little bug, you're coming later tonight for the meal right?"

"Of course, I wouldn't miss it for the world. It's not every day you get to celebrate your bro being accepted to the Royal Air Force."

"Good." He grinned, but a light blush marred his cheeks.

"You're bringing Robyn right?"

Carly grabbed her bag and keys and stood at the door, she smiled back at her family. "Maybe, but only if you behave, she knows your Lothario ways. Good luck bro. Love you guys, see you later."

Carly's anguished cries filled the room as the memory played out over and over through her mind; they still had so much to live for. It just wasn't fair. She couldn't breathe, like a huge weight had settled upon her chest and was constantly pressing down. How can she still be alive if her heart had been ripped from her chest like this? How could she survive like this? Would she ever be able to deal with this grief?

A small squeak sounding throughout the room was the only acknowledgement that someone had entered. Small gentle hands pulled Carly's head onto a lap. Soft words attempted to comfort.

"Carly honey, it's Robyn. Oh honey…I've got you."

Two Days Later

"Carly honey, I've made you a brew."

Carly stared blankly at the curtains in the spare room of Robyn's flat. She had spent the last two days crying and sleeping; unable to function after the death of her family. She hadn't even been home and thankfully Robyn had taken charge and done what Carly was unable to do. Carly hadn't been able to face talking to the funeral directors as well as other jobs that needed to be taken care of. The finality of it all would just send her into a state of emotional turmoil. She wasn't able to function at all.

"Carly, come on honey, I need you to come out and talk to me."

Robyn's voice sounded muffled from behind the door, Carly had the urge to ignore it and go back to sleep, back to being with her family in her dreams. A place where no one could take them away like that van driver had. But she felt guilty, guilty that she had left her best friend to deal with everything. Robyn had been simply amazing since she had collected her from the hospital and had already started the arrangements on Carly's behalf. She knew though, that she would have to face the music sooner rather than later. Throwing the covers back she slid out of bed and reached for the worn blue hooded jumper that was on the chair. Placing the oversize top on, she deeply inhaled the CK one after-shave that her brother had worn. This had been his favourite jumper and had been left in her car. She hadn't needed a second thought as to if she would wear it or not, she had just grabbed it.

Carly opened the bedroom door; she knew she looked a mess.

She hadn't brushed her hair and her eyes were red raw from the constant crying. "Hi." Carly's voice was croaky and she tried a small smile as she reached for the mug. "Thanks."

Robyn smiled back and drew Carly from the room and into the small lounge, her arm around her waist offering all the comfort she could. "How you doing?"

Carly shrugged as she curled up on the end of the sofa, drawing her legs underneath her bottom and sinking into the large hoodie.

"I know this is hard honey, god I can't imagine what you must be thinking and feeling right now, but I'm here ok?"

Robyn waited for Carly to nod and confirm she had heard her words, as much as Robyn wanted to give her best friend time to grieve, there were things that needed to be done and dealt with that only Carly had the authorisation to do.

"You know I will do whatever I can to help Carly, but I need you to come back to me honey, I need your help sorting everything out.

There is only so much I can do, especially with regards the funeral."

Robyn looked over to Carly before taking both their mugs and placing them on the coffee table, reaching out she pulled Carly into her arms as the sobs started again. She knew this would start again the minute she mentioned the funeral, but it was something that needed to be said and be dealt with. All Robyn could do was hold

on to her best friend and let the sobs drain away. Carly's words broke Robyn's own heart.

"I miss them Robyn…so much it hurts. Here." She slapped her palm against her chest, right over her heart. "This hurts so much I can't breathe….god I miss them."

Carly's words disappeared into sobs once again and all Robyn could do was hold on tight. Her own words laced with sadness and tears

"I've got you honey, everything will be ok…I've got you."

✳ ✳ ✳

6 *MONTHS LATER*

Carly pulled the Twix chocolate bar out of her pocket as she sat on the park bench, she was sat in the quiet park just five minutes walk from her workplace .After the morning had dragged she had itched to leave, the stifling atmosphere making her irritable. She felt confined, stuck behind her desk and unable to breathe. Her lunch break hadn't come soon enough, thing was, she had already eaten her lunch mid-way through the morning and had just demolished a large tuna mayonnaise baguette. She constantly felt hungry and nothing she did helped.

She nibbled the side of the chocolate bar and watched a dog chasing a leaf as the wind picked it up and tossed it. Robyn had text her but she had ignored it, unfortunately she had found the empty crisp packets, empty cans of pop and take away containers in her room and she had text to say she was concerned, concerned that Carly's eating had become out of control.

No it hadn't, Carly thought, she just ate when she was hungry and she seemed only to be hungry when she was down, which at the moment was constantly. Carly sighed and licked her fingers, savouring the last of the sweet, melted chocolate.

It had helped ease some of the heart ache for only a tiny moment of time, but then the pain returned if not stronger than before, striking through to the core, no less intensified than the day her world fell apart. She understood the whole 'grief' process took time but she couldn't handle feeling like this, feeling useless and unable to function. Her friends had tried their best to be there and get her out of the house, but with having to sort out the funeral, arrange the sale of her parents' home and then deal with the debt that they had left without telling her, she had ended up taking out a hefty loan to pay everything off, so the last thing Carly felt like doing was leaving the flat.

Robyn had again been amazing, but Carly needed her space and she didn't need anyone making comments about whatever she put into her mouth, it was her body dammit and yes, she had put weight on, but wasn't that expected with grief? Food understood, food didn't judge or expect anything in return and she liked that. It was there if and when she needed it and never complained.

Carly crumpled the chocolate bar wrapper in her hand and then placed it in her pocket, she would give herself a few weeks and then she would try and get back into a rhythm with life. But right now,

Carly couldn't face the world like everyone wanted; she didn't want to, life was just too damn hard. No one understood, they just expected her to get on with things. In other words: forget about her family and the fact they had died in a terrible way, get on with life like a normal person and not affect anyone else's lives. That's all she was at the moment, a hindrance on her friends, so she had alienated herself from them. She felt angry though, angry that they could just forget and not have this pain in their lives. Carly embraced the anger, she preferred it to the pain. Reaching down she collected her handbag and stood, time to get back to work, back to the pitying glances. She reached into her bag and grabbed the bag of crisps she had bought at the same time as the Twix. A small voice in the back of her brain said, *don't eat it, maybe Robyn is right, you don't need it.* She silenced the voice quickly, she did need it.

Food helped...it didn't judge or expect anything, she thought again as she walked through the park.

Food helped.

CHAPTER TWO

5 **YEARS ON**

"Happy Birthday, Tart bag! Now, wakey wakey."

Carly groaned and covered her head with the duvet, her muffled voice only just heard but laced with humour.

"Piss off woman, it's far too early."

"Sod early, it's your birthday. Now get the hell up already."

Carly felt Robyn bounce on the end of the bed and peeked over the edge of the duvet. Faced with the glowing, happy face of her best friend she couldn't help but laugh. Although, it was more like a tired chuckle.

"Jesus Robyn, how can you be so happy this early in the morning?"

Robyn rolled her eyes and waved a birthday card in Carly's face to emphasise her meaning. "Because numbnuts, and I won't say

this again, it's your bloody birthday! So I need you to get your arse up, get dressed and come open your prezzies!"

Carly grinned at the excitement in Robyn's voice and

then laughed as Robyn once again bounced from the bed and smacked her arse through the duvet covers as she went.

"Hurry up woman."

It took Carly less than half an hour to get herself ready for her day. It never did take her long to get ready, Carly was limited to the amount of clothes she could wear as she was of a larger size, well compared to what she was when she was younger. So her choices were jeans, leggings or a skirt. Today she had opted for a skirt with a nice bright yellow blouse. Her life had taken a huge turn and now five years on, the differences and consequences were obvious. Since the death of her family and the aftermath dealing with the huge debt she had been left with in their stead, she had been under a lot of pressure and stress. Carly had always been what you would call an emotional eater, but she had found she had turned to food even more to help her deal with the grief.

It was easy for someone who didn't have such a negative relationship with food to make comments to Carly and she wasn't a stranger to taunts and bullying, but she felt like she was in a vicious circle. Every time she looked in the mirror she would get down and she would immediately turn to food to help her feel better. A chocolate bar here, bag of crisps there; it all added up and wasn't something you could just turn off.

Carly shook her head to dispel the negative thoughts, today was going to be a good day so she would start it well. She threw her hair into a simple bun and headed out to meet Robyn who had a brew waiting in the kitchen.

"Ok, finally you are here." Robyn chuckled and handed over three small gifts, all were wrapped in bright purple, sparkly paper and each had a tag on that said, "Happy Birthday CowBag". Carly grinned.

"You can't open them yet." Robyn slammed her hand down over Carly's to stop her ripping into the paper. "Not until you agree to a short shopping trip once you finish work at lunch."

Carly pouted. "Shopping! Seriously?"

Robyn nodded. "Shopping, so we can get ready for your epic night out."

Carly groaned, then grumbled, "Fine," before Robyn released her hand and let the birthday girl open her gifts. Each was a small simple black box with embossed silver letters on the top. Once Carly had figured out what the words said, she felt tears fill her eyes.

"ASHES TO GLASS" the boxes read. Carly opened them slowly to reveal matching earrings, pendant and ring; each with the signature 8mm round setting in sliver and purple glass. Each glass cabochon had ashes encased within it, they shimmered gold and silver flecks in the light. Carly let the tears fall, she had wanted to have these done ever since her family had died and now her best friend had once again done what she didn't.

"Robyn!" Carly's voice croaked.

"I know you had always wanted them done Carly, they can be with you always now."

All Carly could do was nod as she looked over the jewellery in front of her. This had to be the nicest thing anyone had ever done for her. She owed Robyn so much. Her best friend truly was epic.

* * *

Carly groaned inwardly as she read the text that had just come through. She had only just finished packing up her desk for the day and was more than ready for the weekend to start. She had managed, much to her surprise to get the Friday afternoon off, but giving the sob story that it was her birthday had helped, even though her boss has been shooting her glares all morning. Now it was time to get home and chill before her friends arrived and they went out for the evening.

Twenty Five at last, Carly thought as she packed her diary into her purse, it had seemed like the last five years had dragged and it had sucked big time. Ever since her big brother and her parents had died in a car accident, she had been left to fend for herself, as well as deal with their left over debt. She had been left with nothing and even had to take a loan to pay for the funeral.

If it wasn't for Robyn, her best friend and house mate, she would have fallen into the downward spiral of depression and she doubted she would have survived. Robyn had done more for Carly than anyone could imagine. So after five years of neglect and selfpity, Carly was more than ready to see her birthday as the time to make a change, well that was the plan anyway. It was easier said than done.

From Tart @ 12:25pm
Carly, hurry your arse up!! I want to go shopping!!!
Rxx

This was the other thing Carly didn't want to do but this morning she had agreed to it, in her moment of weakness, aka half asleep, Robyn had pounced. Her friends although supportive were lucky, lucky in the sense that they were bean poles whereas she was as far from that as you could get. In short, Carly was the 'Fat friend' of the group, the one that never got looked at twice and tended to get whispered about, and not in the good way.

Carly knew this from a lot of personal experience and had gotten very good at pretending the jibes didn't hurt and she was excellent at hating what she saw whenever she looked into a mirror.

Not that she did that very often.

Carly's shoulders sagged as she typed a reply to her friend.

To Tart @ 12:27pm
Shopping? Really? I don't really feel like it Robyn.

She grabbed her overly large handbag and threw her phone inside, then pushed her chair under the desk and headed for the lift.

Another peek at her boss's office showed Paul glaring once again.

Chin up, she marched past and down to her friend waiting outside.

Carly could see Robyn as she drummed her fingers on the steering wheel of her blue Fiat 500. After she had climbed into the passenger seat, she smiled at her friend. "Robyn can we please give the shopping a miss," she begged. "You know I hate it, it always gets me down."

Robyn just smiled her cheerful 'I always get my way' smile. "Nonsense Carly babes, we will find you a sexy as hell outfit for our night out." Robyn took a breath. "Besides, we never go shopping Carly, it's about time you got out of this funk and you did promise me this morning."

"Agreed! You caught me at a vulnerable moment Robyn, I would have agreed to anything for a cup of tea," Carly argued. *Sexy outfit*, Carly turned to look out the window, there was no outfit available that would make her look and feel sexy.

With a grin, Robyn pulled the car out of the space, she knew she had won the fight, well she always did. They easily joined the flow of traffic. The sound of the radio playing Ed

Sheeran's 'I See fire' filled the silence as Carly desperately tried to come up with any excuse as to why she should skip shopping, unfortunately none were coming to mind and Robyn had been right, she had made the promise that morning and a good friend didn't go back on a promise, regardless of how out of it she might have been.

Carly used to adore shopping, purchasing new things satisfied that small part that all women have, but now after five years spent cheering herself up using food she was limited to where she could get her clothing. She usually used online stores like 'Simply Be'. It also didn't help that due to her current body shape she looked horrendous no matter what she wore, so jeans and jumpers or large t-shirts was the limit to her wardrobe. Fuck, she hated herself. Carly frowned, then started to chew on her nails. Her focus centred on the skin surrounding her right thumb as she blankly stared out at the scenery that passed by.

"Carly honey, come on, it won't be that bad."

Carly shrugged her shoulders and kept her face turned towards the passenger window, she fought back the tears. "It always is

Robyn, it's ok for you. The perfect size 10. The last time I was that size, I *was* 10."

Carly sighed and turned in her seat, her larger frame making the leather squeak. "I'm 25, overweight, extremely single and in a job that holds zero satisfaction for me. If it wasn't for you, I would also be homeless. There isn't really anything I've just said to get excited about, is there?"

Robyn reached over and took hold of Carly's right hand, tugging it from her mouth, the skin on her thumb already red raw from the chewing. Robyn kept her eyes focused on the road as she steered the car.

"Honey, I am always here for you that will never ever change.

It's wrong your parents and brother were killed, wrong

that somehow they had managed to leave you in financial trouble with no word, but please realise that I will support you no matter what." As they pulled into the car park of the local shopping centre,

Robyn squeezed Carly's hand before releasing it to manoeuvre the car into a space.

"But? I know there is a 'but' in there Robyn, so spit it out."

As Robyn slid the Fiat into a space, she quickly cut the engine and turned in her seat to face Carly.

"But, and it's a big but Carly, I will not agree with your whole self-hate thing you have going on right now. I know you don't see it, but you are a beautiful woman with a heart of gold. I don't know what you see in the mirror but you need to stop hating it. Come on honey, you need to stop hating yourself, it's not healthy, I know you have heard this before but your weight does not define who you are." Robyn slammed her open palm onto the steering wheel. "And those that judge you before they know what an amazing and caring person you are need a smack in their 'Special area'."

Carly turned again to look out of the window, she wanted to run away from the sympathy and pity etched on her best friend's face. It didn't help Robyn could read her like an open book, her voice came out quiet as she answered. "I will try, but it's not as easy as that. I wish it was, I wish I could turn off that particular switch in my head, but I can't."

Robyn nodded, "I understand Chica, I really do. So let's start with an itzy bitzy shopping spree and then tonight we let rip, what do you say?"

Carly breathed in slow and deep before she released in one quick exhale. "Fuck it, you are right." Carly placed her hand on the door handle and pushed it down to open the door. "Let's go."

CHAPTER THREE

The music pulsed, the beat so loud it made your chest hurt and your ears ring, the drinks flowed and Carly couldn't help but smile wide as the waiter placed the next round of drinks onto the table. They had been seated within the VIP section of club and had been given drinks for free. They each quickly grabbed a glass and raised them high in the air.

"Carly our chica!! We love you girl, Happy Birthday!"

Carly kept smiling and raised her glass in response, then followed their actions and downed the shot, the harsh liquid burned as it ran down her throat, but then instant warmth replaced the burn as it hit her stomach and added to the already growing buzz she was getting.

There was no way she was unable to smile when she was out with these lot, they always managed to pull some stupid stunt whilst they were hammered. Only this time, Carly would be joining in and not sitting to the side because she was the driver. They hadn't drifted apart since school like most people do, they had made a pact to always keep in touch. Friends like that were a rare find and Carly was lucky to have them in her life.

"We dancing or what? Come on, I bloody love this song!" Hayley shouted out, her voice a near screech as she tried to be heard as Bruno Mars 'Uptown Funk' started and instantly filled the dance floor. Her hands already in the air, she headed straight for the dance floor. The rest didn't need much encouragement and as one they squealed and weaved their way in and out of the crowd to join her. The club, even though it was still early, was filling up quickly and the dance floor had become rammed. Head down, Carly tried to fight her way to the dance floor, on occasion she had to shout over the music to be heard just to get past, which garnered more than one shitty look in her direction. Shouts and grunts erupted to her right as an argument started, bodies jostled and more than one slammed into her. She pushed back and again tried to make it to the dance floor. Just as she was about to step onto the lit up floor she was pushed by a firm body, her own tumbled to the

floor as multiple drinks from the fight coated her from head to toe as she hit the deck.

Robyn was the first by her side, regardless of her skimpy outfit she bent down to help her friend.

"Shit Carly, are you ok honey, are you hurt?"

Carly shook her head and looked down at the mess that was her outfit. Robyn looked furious as she shouted to the lads that had been fighting. There were more than five of them, all good looking but arrogant in their attitudes. They sneered as they looked down at Carly, still on the floor and soaked in their spilled alcohol.

"Yo Shitheads, watch where the fuck you are pushing people!"

Robyn turned to help Carly, making sure her final insult was heard,

"Bellends."

Robyn helped a soaked and now shaken Carly to her feet, she hobbled slightly and she realised that she had twisted her ankle on her way to the floor. She winced and tried to fight back her tears. Her brand new outfit was now ruined, her purple blouse had multiple stains and it now reeked of alcohol and her blue jeans had red and yellow staining across the lap, making her looked like she had wet herself. She dreaded to think what her hair and makeup looked like now, she knew without a doubt this was the end of her evening.

Unfortunately the night was about to get a hell of a lot worse.

The group of lads that had caused the drama turned again and laughed at her sodden appearance, then they spotted Robyn and started to whistle.

"Hey darling, don't blame us maybe your friend here should have stayed at home. Can't you see the damage an arse her size can cause?" He snorted and his mates soon joined in as they openly made fun of Carly's size. Robyn fought back a growl as she turned to face them, hands on her hips.

"You. Fucking. What!!!" Her voice seemed to get higher in pitch with each syllable.

Carly grabbed Robyn's arm, "Robyn, leave it honey. I'm going to head home, please don't make a fuss."

Robyn turned only slightly and growled more, "No Carly, I will not just leave it, I want these arsewipes to apologise, and don't you dare go anywhere."

The rest of Carly's friends had arrived to back up Robyn as she faced down the men. Carly hated that everyone was starting to look at them, most people had moved away and now there was a circle surrounding them and all she wanted was a large hole to open up and swallow her down. She knew they would say things about her size and right now she couldn't deal with it.

The leader of the group of men stepped forward, he would have been gorgeous if it hadn't of been for the cruel smirk that was plastered on his face. He ignored Carly, but looked Robyn up and down and of course liked what he saw.

"Honey, we aint apologising for shit." He pointed his finger right towards Carly. "That fat cow got in our way, so put up or shut up sweet heart."

He grinned back at his boys before he continued and again stepped forward, his hand reached out to touch Robyn's face. "You should be thanking us." Carly watched as Robyn smacked his hand away.

"Us boys were watching you and your *other* friends and liked what we saw, but your fatty friend here was putting us off…" Carly didn't wait for him to finish or for Robyn's response, she took the coward's way out and bolted towards the exit. The look of pity on the faces of the other clubbers faces hurt. She could hear her friends call out, begging her to stay but she couldn't. Tears streamed down her face as she smashed her way through the exit, her breaths came in big gasps. Her feet hit the pavement and she bolted to the taxi rank in search of a lift home. Her ankle hurt like hell and once she was free and out of sight of the club she slowed her pace.

Fed up was a complete understatement. Carly walked the short distance to the office of the taxi company, the events of the night going round and round in her head until the upset and pain were washed away by her tears, only to be replaced by intense anger.

"How fucking dare they!" She clenched and unclenched her fists continuously as she entered the office of the taxi company. The small attendant behind the counter seemed alarmed at her appearance and anger, but Carly didn't care, she had had enough. How dare they treat her like that, yes she wasn't perfect but nobody was. She knew her faults better than anyone, but she didn't appreciate being judged by people that didn't know her, didn't know why she had let food dictate her life for the past five years. They didn't know why she struggled on a daily basis.

Carly turned to look out of the window, the lights of other clubs illuminated the streets as well as the headlights of cars passing on the road. But one light stood out, bright and clear. Carly wiped the tears from her face and lifted her chin, she felt something snap inside, almost like a light bulb moment and she embraced it. She cancelled the taxi and headed back outside and towards the beckoning lights.

Change was happening and it was starting right now!

Just watch this fucking space…

CHAPTER FOUR

1

4 MONTHS LATER
WEDNESDAY 9TH FEBRUARY

Watching her had become habit, one he never wanted to break. Ever since she had joined the gym, he had been drawn to her. At first it had been how shy she was, but as she had become accustomed to her workouts and used to the gym atmosphere, she had grown in confidence. He had spoken to her a few times and she had been so sweet. Almost coy and he knew what that meant. She wanted him but was too shy to outright ask.

So he watched her at every workout, he watched her in her car, whenever she was at work, positive she positioned herself by the window so she could be seen every time and even when she had taken a shower, he had found a way to watch that too. No one else knew he watched her or even that he took pictures and stalked her Facebook account. But he wanted to know everything about her, so when she became his she would want for nothing.

Surely she knew how much of a tease she was to him, her

smiles intoxicating. He couldn't wait to finally be able to touch her skin and kiss her lips. He had been sending her gifts but she never displayed them like he wanted, he would find them in the bin of the changing room when she had left. But she always managed to leave him gifts in her locker, he knew she left them there just for him. Last night, she had left her panties still damp from her workout. He smiled as he remembered the pleasure he had gotten from them alone.

Yes she wanted him, he knew she did, all he had to do was make it possible for him to have her, an opportunity that he could control. Being careful not to attract attention to himself, he moved to the sit down bike and sat down ready to watch her once again as she worked out.

She would be his, he repeated in his head, over and over.

* * *

"Prick, prick, prick!"

Carly chanted under her breath as she watched her boss walk away from her desk and back towards his office. His smug attitude had always got on her nerves but today it was really rubbing her up the wrong way and then some. What was really pissing her off was his constant comments about her eating habits, no matter what she ate, he always had an opinion about it. It had taken a while but Carly was now in a comfortable routine with her food, she had a better relationship with it now and no longer felt the need to comfort eat like she used to. But being made to feel like she was constantly watched when she ate was giving her a complex again. Carly had worked far too hard for a prick like him to make her feel like she had over a year ago. She could have probably taken any criticism if he had been a picture of health himself, but with balding ginger hair, a hairy chubby face and a beer belly so big she was certain he hadn't looked down and been able to view his own penis since the 1980's, he had little room to talk on any of her eating and gym activities. He was about as fit and healthy as Johnny Vegas and the polar opposite to her trainer, Andy.

Thoughts of Andy always managed to create a feeling of butterflies in her belly, he was like most trainers, ripped and fit but not over the top. What made him different, in her eyes, was that he was a genuinely nice guy. In the time that she had been having PT sessions with him, he had never once put her down or made fun of her size. He had only ever offered encouragement, even when she had fallen off the wagon before she had sought professional help for her eating disorder.

Carly scrolled her mouse over her emails although she wasn't really focusing on the words. She had seen her therapist for an appointment last week and was over the moon with her progress. Having been diagnosed as having an eating disorder had made Carly realise she had help and that she could and would beat it. In her case she binge ate or comfort ate whenever she felt emotionally compromised, this had started when her parents and brother had passed away and it was how her unhealthy relationship with food had begun. Now with the help from Andy and her therapist, Cheryl, she could enjoy food like it was meant to be enjoyed and not used as an emotional crutch. Yes, she had those days where she struggled but compared to where she had been, Carly was now almost free.

"Carly, do you have those papers finished or not?"

Paul's harsh voice cut through her thoughts making her scowl, pushing her chair back she grabbed the afore mentioned papers from the printer and walked to Paul's office. His office was like his person: messy and unorganised. It also held a nasty stench to it that had Carly's stomach rolling with the chance of putting her off her lunch. He sat back in his chair, stomach protruding and held his hands out for the papers. With no words, Carly handed them over, all the while thinking about where she would love to stick those papers, her face muscles had become tired from the false smiles she had to give out. She would love nothing more than to tell Paul where he could shove his job, but she needed the money.

"Are these signed?"

"Yes," Carly grated out.

"Dated?"

"Yes."

"You have checked these for mistakes?"

"Yes," she repeated. "Do you need anything else?"

As she was waiting for his answer, she felt a shiver crawl up her spine as he made an obvious gesture of looking her up and down before he finally answered.

"No, you can go for now."

Carly turned and rolled her eyes, he was a greasy slime ball and a letch, what she wouldn't give to get him in the boxing ring at the gym. That was one workout she had come to adore. Well not the boxing, she was a big girls blouse after all and didn't like the idea of getting hit, but punching the crap out of something helped when she felt frustrated and was perfect to work out those emotions when the sleaze had annoyed her. But to get him in the ring so she could take her aggression out on the actual source would be bloody brilliant. Carly smirked as she walked back to her desk, the daydream itself lightening her mood. Placing her left leg on the chair and then sitting down, she curled into her office chair, if she could she would have taken her shoes off but she didn't want any excuse to have to talk to her boss again and he would no doubt say something.

Clicking on the refresh button she checked through her emails, making sure invoices were forwarded to the relevant persons and any new information or orders were sent to Paul. Placing her chin in her palm she leant on her elbow and looked at the screen, words blurred in and out until one stood out. The sender no one she recognised but strange none the less, the words caused her stomach to flip over and not in the good way.

Sender : IWllMakeYouMine@yahoo.com
Princess
Watching you is the ultimate pleasure for me, we will be together soon.
It won't be long now.

Carly frowned and read it again before moving it to another folder, she wanted to delete it but a gut feeling told her not to. This hadn't been the first strange and random message she had received and to be honest, she was convinced that the sender had just got the wrong person. Well she had thought that before the random flowers and notes had started to appear at the gym. She knew she should have told someone about them, but would someone believe her or just think she was making it up to gain attention? Really, why would anyone want to stalk or harass someone that looked like her, it didn't make sense, so Carly kept quiet and would deal with it if she needed to.

Turning her emails off, she pulled up her documents folder and focused on that and not on the clock, soon, as long as the day didn't drag it would be 4pm and she could leave this hell hole and head to the gym. This job held nothing for her, she felt like the days just ticked by slowly until the weekends or her holidays. Carly sighed rather loudly and then forced a cough, if Paul found out she was bored she dreaded what pathetic jobs he would give her.

As if he had read her mind, Paul's voice called out from his office, she swore he just knew when she didn't want to talk to him and deliberately set out to piss her off.

"Carly!"

"Yes Paul," she called back sweetly, although she wanted to tell him to fuck off.

"Do me a favour and go over to HotSpot for me and grab my lunch, I've ordered it through."

Carly sighed again, Jesus Christ!! If he wasn't commenting on what she ate he was trying to tip her off the wagon by sending her for his lunch, which was always from the kebab shop over the road and it was always the same order: mixed meat kebab with a full salad and a bag of chips, finished off with a bottle of coke. She snorted, Carly saw absolutely no point in the salad, only that she bet it made him feel a smidge less guilty of the crap he was constantly pumping his body full of. It made her think though, as it hadn't been that long ago she was doing exactly what he was now. She grabbed her coat from the back of her chair and her phone before she walked back to his office. With a grin, he threw a twenty pound note her way.

"Don't take too long." He smirked and patted his belly. "I'm wasting away here."

Carly forced a fake laugh and turned away, his voice followed her, "There should be enough there to get yourself something if you want, I know eating that rabbit food of yours can get boring."

Carly gritted her teeth and counted to ten before she replied,

"Thanks Paul, but I'm good, thank you." Why was he such a twat!

"Your loss, Carly."

Carly's jaw had started to ache from the constant fake

smile she was always having to use around her boss, he was irritating and a complete arsehole. She pulled her phone from her pocket the moment she exited the building, hitting speed dial to the one person who would understand her plight and cheer her up. It answered on the third ring.

"CowBag! What's up?"

Carly laughed. "Hey tart, just wanted to call and hear a voice that wasn't Paul's."

"Ahh, the douche has stepped up his fucktardary then."

Carly nodded even though Robyn couldn't see her. "Uh huh, big time."

"What did he do?"

Carly sighed and stopped at the side of the road, waiting for the best time to cross, the nearest crossing was halfway down the road and the mood she was in, she really didn't want to traipse all the way there and back. "Well, I am currently on my way to HotSpot to collect his lunch order for him, after I have spent all morning doing his typing and invoices for him." Carly paused, then remembered his parting comment. "Oh and he said I ate rabbit food and that I could buy myself something with the change if I wanted."

Carly grumbled and continued on, "I swear he does it to see if I cave and then he has bragging rights that I can't stick to anything and can make me feel like a disappointment."

Carly waited for the eruption on the other end of the phone, that was what usually happened when Carly told Robyn about Paul's behaviour. Only this time the eruption never happened.

"Well, what a git," Robyn stated calmly, her sigh matched that of Carly's earlier.

"Git! Robyn that's, well, that's lame for you. Are you ok?"

Carly heard Robyn move, from the sounds she was making she had moved from her chair, her heels loudly clicked across the tiles in her office, the door closed followed by more footsteps and then another door. Finally Carly heard traffic so she knew Robyn had stepped outside.

"Your Boss, Carly, is the biggest NumptyFuck originated from the town TwatVille and if I ever get my hands on that fucknugget he will need tweezers and a straw, along with a piece of cheese to ever locate his cock ever again."

Carly snorted as Robyn let rip, she may have the looks and actions of a well-bred lady but when needed, she could produce the most colourful language ever to erupt from a woman's mouth. But when you are brought up spending most of your time hanging around with a Sunday league football side then you are bound to pick up on a few things.

"Is that better and more to your standards, Carly?" she said sweetly.

"That's so much better," Carly laughed. "Don't worry about the falling off the wagon, he won't win. I don't want or need a kebab."

"Honey, are you sure? I know some days you struggle." She paused. "I know you lick the wrappers from my chocolate bars and sniff my food when I'm not there," she said in a mock serious voice.

Carly laughed hard and moved to cross the road. "Fuck off, and yes I am sure. I do not do that and I only lick the wrapper of the chocolate bars if they have melted to it, I am allowed a treat now and again you know."

Robyn laughed on the end of the phone, her husky laugh- Carly had little doubt- would be gaining looks in her direction. "That's my girl, I believe in you. Right, I need to talk to you about something and I don't think it can wait till later."

"Uh oh, is that your serious voice Robyn?"

"Shut your face and listen ok?"

Carly nodded again, forgetting her friend couldn't see her.

"Yeah go on."

"I know you hate your job and you hate your douche of a

boss just as much, I'm amazed you haven't been headhunted before considering you practically run that place but I digress." Carly smiled as she listened to her friend, she was fiercely protective and for that, Carly would be forever grateful. There had been a time when she doubted that she would have survived if it hadn't of been for Robyn. Her friend continued to talk.

"Well you know I've been busting my arse at work, gaining new clients and new contracts, well I am now that busy work have finally given me the budget for a Personal Assistant, aka a Biatch."

Carly stopped walking and held her breath. "Robyn, what are you saying?"

"Carly, my little wench, go tell your boss where he can shove his job and come be my PA. The wages are more than you are on now and you will be busy, but I guarantee you won't get treated like

shit."

Carly was stunned; she didn't know what to say. For so long she had wanted out of that boring job, but with only 'Office Assistant' on her CV, getting a better paid one was difficult. But Robyn had once again come to the rescue. A loud horn pulled Carly from her thoughts and made her realise she was stood in the road. She waved an apology to the driver and stepped onto the pavement.

"Robyn, are you serious?" Carly asked, her voice squeaky.

"Damn right I am, I need you to be my assistant honey. You have serious organisation skills along with an unhealthy dose of

OCD. You are perfect for the job."

Carly couldn't breathe, she felt dizzy, like she had stood up too fast only she was already standing.

"Robyn, give me five minutes and I will call you back." Without waiting for a reply, she hung up and walked over to a bench that sat in front of the few shops present. Carly flopped onto the seat and just looked at her mobile phone. Her background picture looked back at her, a picture of Robyn and herself sat at the beach taking a selfie. She owed this woman so much already, but there was no way she could turn it down. Not only would it get her out of her current hell hole but give her more money so she could live life better. The pro's far outweighed the cons, but the question remained: was Carly brave enough to take the leap? Flicking her thumb across the screen, Carly called Robyn straight back.

"Carly! You pulled up your big girl panties or what?"

Robyn's voice sung across the line, Carly couldn't help but grin as she answered.

"Robyn, you've just got yourself a PA, I hope you realise what you have just gotten yourself into."

Carly heard Robyn whoop over the phone. "You won't regret this Carly, I promise you that."

Laughing and feeling a lot lighter than she had done before, she stood and walked towards The HotShot Kebab shop. "Carly, you want me to come and help you tell the douche?"

"Oh hell no, that pleasure is definitely all mine."

"Aww, Carly that's not fair." Carly didn't doubt that Robyn was pouting.

"Don't pout Robyn."

"Am not."

"Yes you are, you always pout that's how I lost out last week at the cinema. You pouted so we would go see 'Me Before You' when I wanted to watch the new Ninja Turtles film."

"Whatever, I don't pout. Now piss off and let me work. I have paperwork to fill in regarding a batshit crazy new employee." Carly laughed again. "Don't work too hard and thank you

Robyn, for everything."

"No Carly, thank *you*, I don't think I could trust anyone else to have my back."

Carly smiled. "Always Robyn, that's what best mates are for."

Robyn snorted "Sod best mates, you are my sister." She paused. "Love you, lard arse."

"I love you, tartbag."

CHAPTER FIVE

ndy looked at his watch then looked at his phone; 4:30pm and right on time. He smiled as the expected text came through.

Carlyxx @ 4:30pm
Bossman
We still on for PT on Friday?
FYI no Freddo in 8 weeks.
Carly

He laughed, every week without fail Carly would text him to make sure he was ok for their PT session and every week he would reply the same answer. How could he say no to her? She didn't know it, but he looked forward to their workouts. He looked forward to the banter that had become the norm between them. When he looked back, he couldn't remember ever being happier than when he was with her in the gym. There was just something about Carly that called out to him, made him realise he wasn't the only one that had battled their own demons.

Placing his phone back on the desk after replying to her text, he thought back to his own past, everyone had their own shit but his ran deep. Most looked at him and thought he had had it easy, that life had been a walk in the park and that he had been gifted what he had. None knew he had fought tooth and nail for everything and that if it hadn't of been for one man, things would have been very different.

His early years, up until he was four weren't something he looked upon fondly, and a lot of it he had blocked out. It had taken years of specialised counselling to get him to the point he didn't have an anxiety attack at the mere thought of them. Most of his early years he had watched his brute of a father beat seven bells of shit out of his mother. He would sit in the corner and listen to her cries as she begged him to stop. But one night his father didn't stop, he just kept going until the only sounds that remained were the harsh breaths of his father and the sound of fists on pummelled flesh. Not much had remained of his mother's face and Andy had been petrified, that much he could recall with clarity. He had done what any normal person, never mind child would have done, he had ran. In just his nappy he had bolted down the street in the autumn cold weather until a police officer had found him and questioned the blood splatter that had coated his body.

Andy sat back in the chair and let the memories flow, they no longer haunted him like they had. It was the past and the past couldn't hurt him. After they had arrested his father, Andy had been passed around from grandparents to uncles and aunts until finally, his great uncle David had agreed to take him in when all others had decided a traumatised child was just too much like hard work for them. So he had been officially adopted by uncle David at the age of five and he had been all the family Andy had needed. David had been patient when Andy cowered every time David raised his voice, he had dealt with every nightmare and had attended every counselling session, proving to Andy that he was nothing like his father.

David had been a retired SAS army officer and ran his house like he had his command, strict but with purpose. Andy had revelled in this as he grew older, preferring the strict routines to his day. This had been what he had needed and it had quickly become his therapy. As soon as Andy had hit 16, he had asked permission to enrol in the army. His uncle had inspired him to become a better man and he wanted to make the man that had given him a second chance at life, proud. So with David's full support they had made an appointment and had met with an Army recruitment officer.

Andy sighed as he looked out over the gym and rubbed his chest, lost in his own memories. His dream of joining the Army had been quickly squashed as he had been informed he was too young to join and his medical condition meant he was ineligible. Andy had been gutted, he had been born with a recurring Pericarditis, which was the inflammation of the fluid sac that surrounded his heart.

Although not fatal, it drastically messed with Andy's dreams and plans for the future. But always the supportive role model, David hadn't let him dwell on what most would think as a failure. He had noticed Andy's love and interest in exercise and had encouraged Andy to train and become a personal trainer, that way he could easily continue with a strict regime and focus on helping others. All the while getting constantly checked to make sure his health was tip top. By the time Andy had hit 20 he had been a fully qualified PT for two years and he was one of the most sought after PT's in the area. His uncle had always said he would be ten times the man that his father was and he hoped he lived up to that expectation.

Unfortunately his uncle David had passed away four years before; it had hurt to lose him. He never really mourned his mother as he felt he never knew her, but

David… he had struggled with the pain of losing the one man he could look up to and go to when he needed advice. He had sought help not long after, worried his old nightmares would re-surface. He had surprised himself with how well he coped and had come out the other side stronger. That was probably one of the reasons why he felt a connection with Carly the way he did.

His uncle had left Andy a small inheritance with the sole purpose of fulfilling his dream, David had known that Andy had wanted his own gym and had given him the means to do it. Even from the grave that man had helped Andy and he hoped now, he was proud. Proud of the man he had finally become. And nothing like the one that had sired him.

One thing his father had taught him though, was how not to treat a woman. He would rather take his own arm than ever lift a hand to hurt a woman, especially one that he loved. Andy ignored the pang in his heart at the thought of love, as with life the affairs of the heart were a roller coaster and sometimes you had to go through the hard times before you hit the good. Andy laughed to himself, if anyone heard the romantic crap he had running through his head he would probably lose his man card. To be honest, he didn't care.

Sitting back up in his chair he focused back on the computer and the staff schedule he was working on, he had to stop delving back into memory lane but sometimes he needed to go back to his roots to realise what he needed now.

His thoughts once again returned to Carly and how he felt about her. She was easily someone he would be happy to annoy for the rest of his life, but he didn't know if she felt the same. But he reckoned he would enjoy finding out.

CHAPTER SIX

F**RIDAY 11*TH* FEBRUARY**

Today had been a good day, after her conversation with Robyn on Wednesday, Carly had waited until the Friday to drop the bomb on Paul "floppy chops" Smith, as Robyn liked to call him. Personally she knew how much those jibes hurt and had told Robyn as much. But every time she had broached the subject of weight with Paul, he had gotten really arsy and proved that he didn't want help. He was happy in his bubble, slowly killing himself with his lifestyle choices.

She had been there and there was no way she was going back.

The day had been planned, go into work as usual, act all innocent and then, bam! Drop the bombshell at lunch after all the jobs were done and leave, never to return. Robyn had said she was being too nice in doing the jobs, but she couldn't just leave them. It was like her OCD needed them done or she would start twitching.

So she had done her jobs and calmly walked into Paul's office, leant against the door frame and waited for him to finish his call. "Yes, yes I will have those done for you before 4pm," he cooed on the phone. She smirked as he had yet to see her. He wouldn't be getting those papers done because she wouldn't be here to do them.

She watched the sweat bead on Paul's brow as he continued to suck up to, she assumed, the company director on the end of the phone. He was the only man above Paul that could make the man sweat like he was doing a hard cardio session when he was stationary. Carly, with any other person felt mean with what she was about to drop on Paul, but he had been such an arsehole towards her that she felt more like the human version of Karma getting even.

She watched him put the phone down and turn in his chair and waited for him to notice her standing there. Before he had time to scowl, Carly recognised the look of worry that crossed his face, but that did nothing to move her from doing what she had waited so long to do.

"Ahh Carly, have you done that paperwork I gave you this morning?"

"Yes Paul, all finished and emailed over as well as the hard copies filed, emails answered and invoices sent to accounts as well."

He huffed as he pushed his large belly up against the desk in an effort to move closer. "Well I obviously haven't given you enough work to do then if you have time to stand at the door."

Carly held up a hand to stop him. "Firstly Paul, it's lunch and you don't pay me for lunch so I can stand where I bloody well like."

She watched his face change colour slightly as he wasn't used to being spoken back to.

"Secondly, this…" She held up a letter in her hand, "is my letter of resignation, effective immediately." She watched more as his mouth opened and closed in shock, so she continued stopping him from saying anything. "In this letter is my full resignation and my reasons why, I have included a detailed diary spanning the past few years of the work I have done and what you have not."

Carly noticed Paul's face grow redder and redder before he stood and knocked over his chair. "WHAT?"

She calmly continued, "Also included are the notes of every time you have made a derogatory, sexist remark about me as well as the sexual innuendos and advances you have made."

"WHAT?" he repeated, and all Carly could do was smile, especially when he went to tear up the letter.

"Err, I wouldn't do that." Paul stopped mid tear and looked at her, his face full of anger. "You see, I may have emailed the entire letter to your bosses as well." She shrugged. "Thanks for being the worst boss ever and well, yeah, laters!!" Carly smiled wide, turned and walked away. Today was definitely a good day and Robyn would be so proud.

* * *

"Carly, come on girl give me five more," Andy called out, pulling Carly from her inner musings as she went into the squat position, legs bent, back straight, arse out to dead lift the 80kg bar. Sweat poured down her face and had soaked into her vest top. She was unable to hold back the grunts of effort and strain as she finished off the reps in her last set. Andy, when in this mood, was pure evil especially when it came to her personal training sessions. He seemed to take a great amount of pleasure in causing her the most amount of pain in the gym. The noises that erupted from her mouth were almost embarrassing, but then again most of the other people in the gym made similar ones. Carly couldn't really complain though, she felt like she owed Andy a hell of a lot more then what she paid him and she would happily take the beasting any day. She smiled as he threw her a bright purple water bottle before he started clearing up the weights. She wiped her head with the back of her lifting glove and thought back to the day she had first met Andy.

He had been the trainer on shift that night when Carly had marched in half drenched from the booze that had been launched at her. Her hair and makeup had been a mess but he had taken one look at her face and knew she had meant busi-ness. He had genuinely seemed to understand her frame of mind and even got pissed when she had told him what had happened. He never once made her feel large or fat and had even gone as far as to give her a small taster session.

Andy had handed over a set of boxing gloves and lead her over to the boxing ring where he had let her beat all her anger out on him and his pads. She had pummelled the ever loving crap out of those pads, letting every harsh word, every derogatory look and every feeling of self-guilt over not fitting in out on those two small pads. It took only ten minutes of using the pads for Carly to realise what she wanted and it had opened her eyes, she needed to make a change. No more self-pity and definitely no more self-guilt, that chapter of her life was now over.

"Carly, enough with the catching flies, go and bloody cool down before I make you do burpees."

Carly pulled her thoughts back to the present and grinned at

Andy before she saluted. "Why yes, El-Cap-itan."

"Smartarse, don't make me punish you," he laughed, before he turned back to the weights, re-racking them with ease. Carly couldn't help but take a few seconds to admire what had to be the most perfect, tight arse ever to grace the UK. It was hard not to admire Andy, he was annoyingly perfect in every way as far as she was concerned. He obviously had the body of a god as he practiced what he preached, she had seen him doing solo workouts when the gym had been empty and he had removed his top. Carly had to bite her lip as she remembered watching all that muscle flex. It wasn't just his body though, he was just a nice guy, he wasn't arrogant or up his own arse and actually gave a shit about his client's health and wellbeing. He had never once taken the piss out of her for her size or weight, and when she was even unable to do one push up he had just encouraged her and helped her improve. For that she would always be grateful. It was those reasons that she kept her distance with regards to their personal lives. She had never asked if he was single; one, because she would be gutted if he wasn't, and two, she didn't expect a guy as gorgeous as him to be interested in a Plain Jane like her. Self-doubt would always rear its ugly annoying head with its 'he would never like you anyway'.

As her thoughts swirled here and there she had set herself up on the sit down bike, her legs circled in a steady motion, the speed constant and her heart rate slowly reduced to its normal beat. This was what she now thrived on, no longer a slave to her food binges, she battled her inner demons in the gym and she always hit them hard.

"CARLY!" She grinned more as her name was shouted from across the gym. "Stop grinning, as soon as you have done your ten minutes cool down get your arse to the consult room. It's D-Day."

Carly dropped her head so her chin touched her chest and groaned, time to weigh in, this was the part that always panicked her. She hated facing those scales. Old habits die hard. She smiled again though, she had beaten them, it may have been only a pound at a time but by god they hadn't gotten the best of her.

Carly finished her cool down on the bike and stretched off. Andy had always taught her the benefit and need to stretch and as such, she had been lucky to not suffer from any injuries as yet. She again grabbed her signature bottle and headed to the small consultation room that was located near reception, the changing rooms and Andy's office. She had come so far and was determined no matter what the scales said, today she would be happy.

As she walked in he looked up from his clip board. "You stretched?" his calm deep voice asked. Carly nodded and started to remove her trainers. For a moment she just stood there and looked down at the scales as if scared to go near them.

"Come on trouble, let's get this over with." Andy smiled his encouragement as Carly stepped onto the scales and closed her eyes, head tilted up so she couldn't even peek. After a few moments of silence, Andy's voice filled the room.

"WHOOP!! Get the fuck in!!"

Carly's eyes snapped open and she looked across to Andy. "What?"

He continued to grin like a Cheshire cat as he wrote on his chart, his head nodded towards the scales. "Take a look and see for yourself."

Carly looked down at the numbers, she tried to make sense of them but her mind had gone blank.

"Five stone Carly!" He grinned again, this time giving Carly his full beam wattage smile, one that included dimples.

"Baby, you've done it." Carly still hadn't twigged and watched as he dropped the clipboard and swept her up into a huge hug, he spun her around as he laughed. Her mind instantly focused on the fact she was in his arms and surrounded by his strength as well as his warm, earthy scent. The feeling of his solid body against hers was almost distracting but then it hit her. Five stone...shit, she had lost five stone in weight.

Carly couldn't help herself as she finally gave in and squealed her delight, she wrapped her arms around Andy's neck and returned the hug full force. They both continued to laugh and he continued to spin them in a circle. Carly couldn't help but start to tear up, never in her adult life had she been able to have someone physically lift her as easily as this wonderful man had just lifted her. They stayed like that for what Carly felt was hours when only a minute had passed, but all too soon he slowly let her slide down his body until her feet hit the floor, his arms though remained around her waist. His voice deep, he looked into her face a proud smile upon his own.

"Well done baby, I am so damn proud if you."

Carly beamed as she looked up at Andy's face and met his gaze, his baby blues sparkled and drew her in. This man had become so integral to her she would be lost without him now.

In the 14 months that he had trained her they had bonded, about six months in she had broken down completely. He had already known about certain things but one night she had let it all out. Nothing had been held back. In that moment when most people would have patted her on the back and said 'I'm sorry', he hadn't. Andy had laid his own secrets and hidden demons for her to see. After that night they had become closer than she had been with anyone but Robyn. That had been the day she had known this man held a part of her heart and if he had asked, she would have handed it to him with bows and ribbons on. She knew he was a professional but every now and again she would catch him looking at her and smiling, or they would touch and for a brief moment in time it would be just the two of them, butterflies would erupt and then it would end. In those brief periods of time, Carly was convinced that he felt the same way as she did. Only it seemed neither one of them would make that move.

This was one of those moments, one that would end far too quickly, but she savoured it like she did her Freddos.

"Thank you so much Andy, I couldn't have done this without you. You helped me gain the strength and you kept me focused."

His large hands moved so they sat on her hips and he continued to smile down at her, his eyes never left her face. "Oh Carly, you did all the hard work. You did and no one else. You are so much stronger than you think you are."

In an unexpected move, Andy leaned forward and pressed his lips to her own, the briefest of touches before he removed his hands and stepped away. Carly felt herself blush and she opened her eyes, totally unaware that she had closed them. Andy stood just out of arms reach, he had collected his clipboard from the floor and was just standing there smiling at her. She felt herself blush even more, she couldn't help it. Andy had been her crush now for a while and without knowing it, he had just made one of her dreams come true.

"Go get yourself sorted Carly, you can't celebrate reaching your goal here."

To try and hide her obvious blush, Carly laughed as she bent to collect her Nikes. "Sure thing bossman, same time next week?"

"Yeah definitely, and well done again Carly."

With a full beaming smile, Carly slotted her feet back into her Nikes and grabbed her water bottle. She found it strange that he had all of a sudden stopped using his nickname for her. Usually he always called her trouble but now he had stuck to her name and his voice had dropped in tone; its depth had made her shiver. She wasn't entirely sure why he had called her 'baby', but she liked it because he was the only one to call her that.

"Goodnight Andy."

Without a needy backwards look, Carly raced towards the changing room to grab her handbag from the lockers, in her bid for speed she nearly rebounded off one of the other trainers.

"Oh shit Simon, I'm so sorry," Carly rushed out as she tried to collect herself from slamming into Simon's chest. Just like Andy, he was a good looking guy with a fabulous body; he had brown eyes and dark blonde hair. She had seen him in action a few times when he had to take over Andy's PT sessions due to unavailability and she hadn't wanted to miss a week.

"Whoa there princess." He smiled and steadied her by grabbing her shoulders and squeezed. "Where you off to in a hurry?"

Carly smiled brightly up at the handsome face of Simon, he held her gently and returned her smile as he waited for her to reply. He was better looking the closer you got and had a killer smile with dimples. Unfortunately Carly felt nothing when he turned it on her.

Pity, she thought.

She beamed again. "I hit my goal weight so I want to get home and celebrate," she blurted out.

"Wow congratulations, that's amazing. See, all that hard work paid off," he answered and squeezed her shoulders once again before he leant in with a cheeky twinkle in his eye.

"How about a congrats hug then?"

Without waiting for a reply, he tugged her into his arms and engulfed her into a tight hug, her face pressed into his chest. She couldn't deny he smelled amazing and he was just as solid as Andy. Before letting her step away, he whispered in her ear.

"Want me to walk you to your car?"

Carly chuckled, she stepped back and answered, "That's very kind of you, but I'm good thank you."

Carly could tell he was about to insist, his stance had changed ever so slightly and he looked like he was about to argue, but

Andy's voice cut in.

"Simon, would you go and check in the male changing to see if there is anyone left?"

Carly jumped at the anger in Andy's voice as it called out from behind her, Carly smiled apologetically to Simon who just shrugged in response. Seemingly used to being spoken to in anger.

"Yes sure, you got it," he answered before stepping past Carly, giving a last squeeze to her arm and headed for the men's changing rooms, stopping to look at Andy as he went. The testosterone filled silence made the hairs on Carly's neck stand up. What the hell was wrong with Andy, Simon was only being friendly

There was obvious tension between the two trainers and Carly didn't want to get in between them.

"Thank you" Andy gritted out, his arms folded across his chest.

Carly kept her mouth shut as the two men eyed each other, before

Simon continued on, the door to the men's changing room closing slowly behind him. "Carly, hurry up and grab your gear unless you want to kip here tonight." Andy smiled to soften his words and to make sure she understood he wasn't angry at her. She nodded and bolted into the changing rooms and headed for her locker.

Carly had used the same locker since she had joined the gym and so, as with every visit she unlocked it and reached inside. A flash of red made her squeal and jump back as something fell out of her locker. This wasn't the first time she had found something in her locker, or on her car for that matter. She had thought of telling Andy or one of the other trainers but was convinced they would think she was being silly. A single red rose now lay on the floor and yet another note was taped to the inside of the door, a note that although sweet in its words felt wrong and downright creepy.

Where the hell had that come from? Carly felt spooked and on edge, and not for the first time, it always worried her that someone had managed to get inside her locker. She really should think about telling someone, the messages that she had been getting had been light-hearted but now seemed more possessive. She fished her handbag out and car keys, then as an after thought, grabbed the rose and note. On her way out she threw them into the large bin at the entrance to the changing rooms. They were far too creepy to be taking with her and she didn't want to explain to anyone where they had come from either. Maybe if she just carried on ignoring the notes, emails and messages they would just stop.

Carly practically bounced out of the gym and to her car, the rose quickly forgotten. She definitely earned a cheat meal today, now all she had to do was decide what she wanted.

Oh the decisions!

CHAPTER SEVEN

Andy watched on the CCTV cameras to make sure Carly made it to her car and left without incident. It wasn't a part of his job but he just couldn't help himself when it came to that woman. A huge part of him just wanted to wrap his arms around her, protect her and make sure she was ok at all times.

When she had first come into the gym all that time ago, he had been first struck by her stunning green eyes and full pouty lips. Regardless of her size she had been, and still was, stunning and openly wore her heart on her sleeve.

He had been so angry on her behalf when she had told her story that he had taken her straight into the boxing ring to punch out her anger. When he thought back, that was more for his benefit than hers. He had been sorely tempted to go into that club and beat seven bells of shit out of the lads that had made one so beautiful cry and feel like she wasn't wanted. She had still been dressed in the clothes that had been cruelly trashed; blue jeans and a simple, purple blouse that had been covered in alcohol and she still looked stunning.

As a trainer he would admit, yes, she had been a touch

over weight but she had carried it well. He didn't blame her, in this day and age it was easy to give in to all the quick fix, processed foods.

No sooner had Andy agreed to be her PT and she had joined the gym, she had gained a brand new outlook on life and as expected, had thrown herself into the training and diet with an enthusiasm few ever showed.

Today, he remembered fondly she had finally reached the goal she had set herself, she had dropped five stone and near on seven dress sizes. He couldn't be prouder, but he had expected nothing less from her. His problem now was being able to step back from her. All she would need now were monitoring sessions so she really had no need to be in constant contact. Thing is, Andy had become attached and that was why he broke his own rule in the consulting room. He scrubbed his hand down his face as he watched her drive off, he could see her dancing in her seat a huge smile on her face. This in turn made him smile again and then groan. He had been attracted to her before but now she pulsed with a new found confidence and looked hot as hell and so comfy in her own skin.

She simply outshone any other woman.

Andy thought back to that stolen kiss, because that was what it was. A stolen moment he doubted he would get again. Her lips had tasted exactly as he imagined they would taste like and to finally be able to hold her in his arms, well he had been in heaven. He would have done it a lot sooner if he had known she would have let him.

He wanted her and not just on a sexual level, even though he didn't doubt that would be intense, but she was such a light in what had been such a dull life these past years and he never wanted to lose that. She made him laugh, she was intelligent and she loved her chocolate. By his own rule, dating a client was frowned upon and usually discouraged.

Anyway, he wasn't sure she actually liked him in that way, surely he would have seen the signs if she did.

Andy decided then and there he would find out, a cheeky coffee wouldn't do any harm would it? He would send her a text tomorrow to make sure she was ok, especially after her run in with Simon.

Simon was an issue all of his own, when Carly had first joined the gym he had openly expressed his interest in her which had triggered off a wave of jealously so fierce, Andy was shocked by it. Simon had caused a few issues in the short time he had been here and Andy unfortunately, had received quite a few complaints regarding his attitude towards the male members of the gym. But that had been in the defence of some of the female members, so he had let it slide. Simon was a well liked member of staff. But his actions today had made Andy look like a stupid idiot, all because he was jealous of Simon's arms around Carly. Dealing with staff and people on a daily basis was what happened when you ran your own business and owned your own gym. He smiled with pride, this was his legacy, one he had built up from scratch and he hoped would continue to flourish. His past experience of working for corporate companies had shown him they didn't care about the clients or staff. His hard work may only be like a small drop in the vast ocean but at least he was doing his bit; educating people that a healthy diet and regular exercise would help improve anyone's health. Andy grabbed his keys and locked his office for the night, his thoughts as always returning to Carly. Yeah he had a plan, first thing tomorrow - no! Fuck that, he would do it tonight, he would ask Carly out for coffee.

* * *

Carly was absolutely ecstatic, she had finally reached her goal weight as well as quitting a job she hated and having a fabulous new one to go to. She was now dressed in her fleece Pj's after a steaming hot shower and was snuggled up on the sofa with a large mug of hot chocolate. Robyn had yet to arrive home from work and Carly was dying to tell her friend her good news.

She had already made the decision that they would go clothes shopping the next day, well she had to now. She was the PA for Robyn Andrews, Solicitor extraordinaire, and would have to dress the part. The plan would be to shop and then venture out into town in the evening for the first time since the incident over 14 months ago. Carly hadn't even drunk one drop of alcohol since that night and instead chose to get her kicks from the gym instead. That had paid off in spades and she now felt like a new, more confident woman.

The next day now couldn't come quick enough and she brimmed with energy instead of the outlines of a panic attack and that alone showed how far she had come. All of her hard work and dedication had paid off and she no longer felt like the 'fatty' she used to be called.

Her phone chimed with her favourite Kelly Clarkson song "The

Sun Will Rise" to alert her to a new text. Expecting a message from Robyn, she grabbed her phone.

From Andy Trainer <3 11.05pm
Carly
I know it's late and a long shot, do you fancy a coffee this weekend?
My treat. Andy xx

The text although not from Robyn, was enough to make her beam. Ok yes, she had a major crush on Andy and after his huge hug and oh so tender kiss she felt like she could easily fall in love with the guy. Who wouldn't, he was perfect, well in her eyes he was. It had been a long time since she had let herself even think about dating. Carly refused to get her hopes up though and quickly sent back a response.

To Andy Trainer <3 @11.08pm
Hey Bossman
That sounds epic. Please no beasting though LOL. Is Sunday ok? I have decided tomorrow is my day for shopping and finally going out on the town. I hope you are proud.
Carly xx

Carly hoped and prayed to whatever gods may be listening that this could quite possibly an unofficial date and that he did actually see her as more than just his client. She didn't want to seem over eager and obvious, but having been around him for over a year she felt like she knew him better than anyone. He was one of the only people that knew every-thing from that night of the incident, which is why she was so open about him knowing she was fighting back her demons. She just hoped he was happy about her being like that in her messages. Ahh she was so nervous just texting him. It had been so long since she had done the dating game, if she could even call this that.

From Andy Trainer <3 @ 11.15pm
Carly
That's amazing, you know I am so unbelievably proud of you. You are amazing. Be careful tomorrow night. Sunday is a go.
Andy xx

Carly's reply was almost immediate and as soon as she hit send she regretted being so quick off the mark.

"If that didn't make me obvious I don't know what will," she mumbled to herself.

To Andy Trainer <3 @ 11.15pm
Will do Bossman, have a fab weekend
Carly xx

Carly threw her phone onto the other end of the sofa so she wouldn't keep checking it and relaxed back into the cushions. For the first time in a long while she felt excited about the future and what it would bring. She was happy to be able to get out into the world again. The title of her favourite novel by Melody Dawn swam around in her head. The words "To Live Again" said it all. Carly curled back onto the sofa and got lost in "LadyHawk" on the Classic channel.

CHAPTER EIGHT

S*ATURDAY 12TH FEBRUARY*

"Oh My God!! Carly, you have to try this dress on. It screams 'buy me'," Robyn laughed and threw the spectacularly tiny dress onto the already huge pile of outfits that Carly was carrying around, trailing after her friend. Robyn's version of celebrating Carly's awesome weight loss was a shop till Carly literally dropped session.

Her arms ached and so did her feet and they hadn't even tried anything on yet. Carly didn't remember shopping ever being this exhausting.

When Carly had asked Robyn about the shopping trip, she had barely gotten the words out of her mouth before she had been dive bombed on the couch by a squealing blonde. So here they were, Carly following Robyn around the department store as she picked up every item known to man and placed them into Carly's already over laden arms.

"Chunky butt, come on, we need to try all of these on and then we will need shoes, handbags, oh and you will definitely be needing some new underwear."

"Oi pigeon legs, there isn't anything wrong with my underwear," Carly fired back from behind the mountain of clothing. Their banter always gained looks from other people, but the insults that they fired to and fro had always made her laugh.

"Right yeah, whatever, Mrs granny panties or should I say, belly warmers. Come on Carly, my nan wears sexier panties than you, she even has thongs."

"Ewwww, I did not want that mental picture Robyn, I may actually need mind bleach," Carly snorted, then started to giggle. "I may never look at Nana Phillips the same way ever again."

"My nan rocks and she damn well knows it, come on arse face, hurry up." Carly shook her head and trailed after her best friend, she couldn't help but feel excited, it was damn near infectious. Robyn took this to a whole new level of fun and the constant name calling helped Carly feel less nervous.

"Wench, slow the hell down; I can't see where I'm going. Oh and we can't take too long, I have an appointment at the salon later," Carly shouted, unaware she had basically told the entire store before she followed a bouncing Robyn into the largest cubicle in the changing room.

"Hun, this is the disabled cubicle, we are not meant to use this one." Carly stepped inside and Robyn whipped the curtain closed.

"Carly honey, the store is empty today. I'm sure they will shout at us to move if we need to, besides your arse needs the extra room." Robyn winked and pointed to a small stool to drop the clothes onto. "So, spill! Why are we going to the salon when your hair was only done the other day and looks as per usual, amazing?"

Robyn crossed her arms and looked at Carly with her 'Don't lie to me' face, also known as 'resting bitch face'.

Carly blushed bright red and moved to perch upon the edge of the stool, she fidgeted with her finger nails before she blurted out, "Well, I need my eyebrows and lip waxed as well as my, err, lady garden."

Carly turned in her seat and grabbed a dress, she placed it back on the hanger and waited for her fabulous best friend to start taking the piss.

"Oh wow, my ickle Carly bobs is all grown up and wanting her foo waxed." Carly looked up to see Robyn, she held her hands against her heart and the look that was on her face caused a snort to fire from Carly's nose in a very unlady-like fashion. Her pouty lips almost trembled as she mock cried.

"Fuck off, bony arse," Carly retorted. "Now, help me with these damn dresses already." Robyn grinned and grabbed the first dress, the tight fitting material of the little black dress looked miniscule. Carly was certain she would never get into it, but again realised this was when her demons would surface. They would make her feel like she was that bigger size when in fact, she was so far from it.

"When I'm finished with you honey bunny, you won't even recognise yourself, damn I may even turn gay myself with how good

I'm going to make you look," Robyn winked. "So, kit off lard arse, time for me to be a fucking genius."

"Bossy cow," she fired back as she started to strip.

CHAPTER NINE

"I am so damn hungry my stomach thinks my throat has been cut," Robyn moaned and rubbed her non-existent podge. They had seated themselves at a table and had dumped the numerous shopping bags into a spare chair. They had literally shopped till they dropped and then some. After that, the well expected salon visit had happened. Carly was still feeling the after effects of her treatment and was positive she would be scarred for life. She winced as she gingerly sat in her chair, then wiggled about for a more comfortable position.

"How's the lady garden, chief?"

Carly glared and then leaned back in her chair to read the menu. "No thanks to you, I feel like I've had intimate relations with a damn sand castle. There was no need for you to tell them to wax me completely…like bald." Carly leant forwards towards the table and whispered, "Even back there! Fuck Robyn, that hurt like a bitch.

I nearly kicked the girl in the face."

Robyn cracked up loudly and gained more than a few looks from the other patrons. Carly couldn't help but grin back.

"That's the absolute last time I ask for your help, cow."

Robyn's reply was the simple lift of her middle finger before she buried her nose into the menu.

"Hello, my name is Marie and I will be your waitress today. Can

I get you both something to drink?" Carly smiled up at the young waitress and attempted to not giggle as Robyn moaned at the menu like it was some sort of porn magazine for women.

"Yes thanks, I will have a pint of blackcurrant and soda water no ice, and my obnoxiously loud friend here will have a white wine spritzer." The waitress nodded as she quickly penned the order down onto her note pad.

"Have you been to a Toby Carvery before?"

Carly was about to answer, before Robyn chimed in and stood up. "Have we been? Oh honey, you are about to see something special. Joey Tribbiani has sweet FA on me." Robyn winked at the waitress as she passed and made a beeline for the carvery queue.

Carly smiled her apology at the waitress and watched as she scuttled off to make the drinks. By the time Carly had caught up with Robyn she was already giving her order.

"Brian honey, give me a bit of each, oh and make it the extralarge plate too." Robyn kept a permanent grin on her face as she chatted up the chef whilst he carved her chosen meats.

"God Robyn, I didn't know you were on first name terms with the chefs now, how bloody often do you come here?" Carly chuckled and held out her plate as Robyn glared and moved down the line to fill her plate with veg.

"Just turkey please, Brian," Carly almost shouted so Robyn would hear and smiled her thanks before she followed suit and loaded her plate up with veg.

Once loaded, she headed back to the table and joined

Robyn who, as usual, hadn't waited and was ploughing through her food as if she hadn't eaten all week.

"Good god, slow down woman, I ain't burping you if you get wind." Robyn just stared and slowly placed a fork full of food into her mouth, with a raised eyebrow.

Carly held up her hands. "All right, all right, I'm off your back, you are so bloody grumpy when you are hungry."

Marie the waitress arrived with the drinks and set them down with the usual, "Everything ok with your food?" They both nodded and she raced off again.

Carly's phone then filled the restaurant with 'The Sun Will Rise' as her phone went off. Confused as to who would be texting her as the usual suspect was sat filling her face.

From Andy <3 @ 4.25pm
Carly
How was shopping? Did you have fun?
Andy xx

Carly's face erupted into a full out grin and she quickly typed out her reply.

To Andy Trainer <3 @4:26pm
Bossman
Shopping was exhausting, so was the waxing!! Leg DOMS have nothing on that shit! #ThatBitchHurts LOL.
How was your day?
Carly xx

As soon as Carly had hit send, she started to panic. "Oh Fuck!!

I cannot believe I did that."

Robyn looked up mid mouthful, "Did what?"

Carly blushed and grabbed hold of her glass, taking a large swig as she thought of what to tell her best friend. She had never been brave enough to tell Robyn of her crush on Andy; mainly because she would have encouraged her to act on it. Carly placed her glass down and started to push her carrots around the plate.

"Carly, spill already, it's got to be something juicy 'cos your face is the same colour as my fav hooker red lippy."

Carly looked up to find she had Robyn's full and undivided attention. Bugger!!

"Remember Andy?" Carly asked.

"Oh yeah, Mr Hunky pants who sees to your every gym need and looks like every girl's wet dream." Robyn grinned and waggled her eyebrows suggestively. Carly bristled at her friend's comments, an unexpected wave of jealously hit her. It was so foreign it took her by surprise.

"Robyn!!"

"What!!" she fired back. "He is. I honestly don't know how you concentrate in that place." She sighed and fanned her face. "I would be a drooling mess watching all those muscles flex."

Carly snapped her fingers in Robyn's face to pull her out of her lustful daze. "Focus, tart!" She took a deep breath and blurted the next part out, "Well, I'm meeting him tomorrow lunch time for coffee, no you can't come with me and the reason why I'm about to die of embarrassment is because I may have inadvertently told him I got waxed."

Robyn's eyes grew wide before she snorted then started to laugh. "Oh my god, you didn't? Now that is bloody brilliant." Carly snapped, "You are not helping me feel any better, he's gonna think I'm such a knob and he's definitely going to cancel on me."

Robyn wiped her eyes and sat forward in her chair, the food forgotten as she got a gleam in her eye.

"No he won't honey, because I'm guessing he likes you." She just smiled at Carly, who glared back in response.

"What do you know Robyn? Why are you so sure?" Carly's heart had taken off on a swift gallop at the thought that Andy may just like her in a different way than her being his client. She knew it had been a mistake to persuade her to join the same gym.

"Ok so the gossip on the "gymvine" is Andy has been single for about two years after a particularly shitty break up with a fitness model. SO, because of this he made it his numero uno rule not to date clients." Robyn held up her hand to stop Carly from speaking, "And that includes "coffee". Carly honey, that tells me in itself he likes you more than you think he does."

Robyn grinned and sat back in her chair, the look on her face said 'my work here is done'. "So, has he replied yet?"

Carly simply shook her head and frowned hard, her voice a whisper, "I've blown it, haven't I?"

"Carly honey, give it time, he may just be at work and can't answer straight away."

Carly nodded and looked down at her phone, she was such a dick.

CHAPTER TEN

Andy nearly dropped his phone as he read the text. Waxing!!

What the fuck!! That's all he needed, now he was imaging what she had waxed. Fuck, that alone was able to give him a raging hard on.

Thank fuck his last client had already gone and he was sat behind his desk, hiding from the rest of the gym. Today was what he had nicknamed as Dolly Day. This was because the entire gym seemed to be taken over by skinny blondes with fake tits, who acted like they owned the place and flirted with any bloke around. This also meant his bitchy, two faced slut of an ex-girlfriend would be in.

It was hard to believe that only two years ago he had been convinced she was it for him. He had even decided he was ready to make the ultimate commitment. Well, until he had overheard a few of the regulars talking about her particular skills in the oral department.

He had been completely blind to the fact that she had banged nearly every male member of the gym, and even managed to shag some of the women too. So he sat in his office and avoided the poisonous bitch, kept his door shut and watched the CCTV in case she headed in his direction.

Andy shook his head to dispel the negative thoughts that centred on his ex and focused back on the text from his Carly. His? Yeah he classed her as his, he had done ever since she had walked into his gym. He picked up his phone and reread the message. He wanted a decent comeback and he didn't want to sound like a dick.

To Carly xx @ 4:40pm
Carly
Waxing?? Now I'm intrigued. Still on for coffee tomorrow?
Andy xx

It wasn't his best response to be sure, but that girl had managed to tie him in knots. It had been like that since the start. He really hoped she was still up for coffee; he wanted to spend more time with her and not as her trainer. He knew he was breaking his own damn rule but he no longer cared, he wasn't getting any younger and after two years he was ready to be selfish, and by selfish he meant persuade Carly he was the guy for her.

Andy turned back to his computer, he had best get some more work done and he also had to check out the alarm system as it had been going off randomly at night, that added to his ever growing list of shit that needed fixing. His only enjoyment now was waiting for a text from Carly.

CHAPTER ELEVEN

SUNDAY 13*TH* *FEBRUARY - AM*

Carly groaned as she rolled over and buried her head in her pillows. Her head was throbbing like someone was inside with a full drum set. She squeezed her eyes shut. God, how much did she drink last night? She could remember starting off on a bottle of Prosecco and then there was Tequila. After that, everything was a blur. Carly rolled over again and looked at her alarm clock: 10:35am, God she had slept in later than she ever did. Usually she would be up and out on a run.

"Carly, you awake?" Robyn's whispered, hoarse voice came from behind her bedroom door.

"Yeah I am, just about, come on in honey."

Robyn nudged the door open and gingerly walked in holding two mugs of tea in her hands. Robyn handed one over before she settled on the end of the bed, her legs crossed. Her hair looked like a birds nest and she still had make-up caked on her face. Carly had no doubt about her own post, piss up look and she really, really didn't want to face it yet.

"How's your head?" Carly asked as she wrapped both hands around the mug and held it close.

"Like it's going to explode. How much did we drink last night? I can't even remember getting home."

"A lot by the way I'm feeling. I can't remember much either, especially after watching you doing body shots."

Robyn's eyes went wide. "I did what?"

Carly chuckled and nodded. "Yeah," was all she said. Robyn's face went through a mixture of emotions, from shock at first then embarrassment before finally acceptance. Her answer was to shrug.

"Typical, that would explain why I feel all sticky and why I have some guy's number written on my stomach." She grinned, then winced and placed her palm against her head.

"Best check your phone Carly, I may have done body shots but you were sending Mr. Hottie texts all night."

"What!! I didn't!!" Carly nearly threw her mug in a desperate bid to grab her phone from her handbag on the floor. Robyn reached out and grabbed the mug from Carly's hands and grinned at her friend's panicked expression.

"Oh God, oh God, oh God!"

Robyn snorted as she watched Carly sit on the floor and empty her bag onto the carpet. "You will be saying that and more if you get your way! You do still have that implant right, you know just in case." "Shut up!! He's going to cancel on me for sure now." She eyeballed Robyn. "And yes, the implant is still there, not that I have needed it much."

Carly unlocked her phone and went straight to her messages.

She scrolled up to the last message she remembered getting.

From Andy Trainer <3 @ 4:40pm Carly Waxing?? Now I'm intrigued.

You still on for coffee tomorrow? Andy xx

* * *

To Andy Trainer <3 @ 8:30pm Bossman
Of course I am, and you are not intrigued...just nosey LOL
Off to the club now!! Wish me luck Carly xx

* * *

From Andy Trainer <3 @ 8:50pm
Stay safe Baby, message me if you get bored
And yes I am nosey and my imagination is going mental right now.
;)
Andy xx

* * *

To Andy Trainer<3 @ 9:13pm Really?
Carly xx

* * *

From Andy Trainer <3 @ 9:15pm Have fun, and yes really!!
It would make that pretty face blush if you knew what I was
thinking.
Andy xx

* * *

To Andy Trainer <3 @ 10;30pm
It doesn't take much to make me blush, especially from you LOL
Carly xx

* * *

To Andy Trainer<3 @ 10:45pm
U No U have a Gr8 ass #biteable

* * *

From Andy Trainer<3 @ 11pm LOL Are you drunk already??
Ever wonder why I call you baby?
Be safe
Andy xx

* * *

To Andy Trainer <3 @ 12:30am
I is tipsy.....Cos I'm chubby like a baby
#URHot Cxx

* * *

From Andy Trainer<3 @ 1am
LOL
Very Cute
G'night Carly Andy xx

* * *

To Andy Trainer<3 @ 2am
Andy I...drunk... Loved that kiss
Wouldn't mind more...

* * *

To Andy Trainer<3 @ 3am
Home...safe...

* * *

From Andy Trainer<3 @ 7am
Oh baby, I wish I had been there to see your drunken antics.
Regarding that kiss I assure you I would like more and I intend to
get more.
See you at 1 for our coffee.
Andy xx

Carly groaned and placed her head in her hands, how fucking embarrassing. She glared up at her best friend as she started to laugh.

"Can it Robyn, it's not funny."

"Well, at least he wants to still meet with you and he wants another kiss as well." Robyn started to giggle as she climbed off the bed and placed the mugs down before she pulled Carly to her feet.

"Come on fat ass, time to get you ready for your coffee date."

Carly groaned again and followed Robyn. She was going to need a miracle to make herself look and feel great and right now, she was too nervous about the date as it was.

CHAPTER TWELVE

ndy checked his phone again, it was 1:10pm and Carly still hadn't made an appearance, she hadn't sent a text either. Strange how he was panicking about her not showing up. Was she embarrassed about the messages from last night? He hoped not, because he had loved receiving them. It had made him less worried about her being out, knowing she was too busy texting him to bother with being chatted up. Well that's what he kept telling himself. In fact he had sat desperately waiting on each message and tried to stop himself from getting jealous about how many other guys would see her and want her. It had taken every ounce of will power he had to stop himself from getting changed and heading out to meet up with her.

"Andy?"

Her gentle voice called to him from behind and he turned slowly, a huge smile on his face. She was simply stunning, dressed in faded skinny jeans, ankle boots and a baby blue, long jumper.

Her light brown hair had been tied into a messy bun. Her eyes, although tired, sparkled as she smiled back.

"Hey baby, you had me worried for a moment there. I

thought for sure you were going to stand me up." He watched as a blush climbed up her neck to her cheeks.

"Sorry I'm late, I had to get myself sorted from last night. I'm, err, really sorry about those texts, I honestly don't remember sending them."

Andy grinned and stepped closer, he reached out and grabbed her hand and breathed in her unique scent of lavender. Sweeping his thumb across her knuckles, he loved that her voice sounded husky from the night's excesses.

"Don't apologise, I loved getting them. They made me laugh." She blushed more as he leant forward and placed a kiss on her cheek, then whispered into her ear.

"I loved the fact you admitted to enjoying our kiss." He stepped back, but kept her hand within his own. "Come on, time for some coffee." He winked and tugged her hand, pulling her into the coffee shop.

* * *

Carly's heart was going at a rate of knots, her nerves were shot to hell and she knew her face was the colour of a tomato. Hell, her whole body was on fire just from the feel of his hand on her own. It was strange though, whenever she was near Andy she felt a sense of belonging. As he tugged on her hand and practically dragged her into the coffee shop, she took her time to look her fill. She had never seen him in 'normal clothes' and she was glad.

He was a distraction, dressed in low slung jeans that cupped his arse to perfection, topped off with a fitted white long sleeved tshirt. The material clung to every muscle and tempted Carly with every flex. If she didn't concentrate she would be caught with her tongue hanging out as she drooled.

She had said he was the whole package before, but seeing him like this was like her own personal porn show.

The coffee shop was quiet, so service was quick. Carly had opted for a large hot chocolate with whipped cream and marshmallows, whilst Andy had gone for a simple espresso. They sat to start with, in pleasant silence and every now and again they would smile at each other. Carly was the first to pluck up the courage to speak.

"How's the gym?"

He smiled back and answered, "The same as it was Friday." His smile turned into a grin. "Nothing exciting has happened and I've left

Connor in charge today."

Carly sipped her drink as Andy continued with talk of the gym, their conversation flowing easily. She felt like she could talk to him about anything and not worry about being judged.

"Out with it Carly I can see you are sitting on a question, your leg's been tapping for a good five minutes now."

Carly took a deep breath in and then released it slowly; all the while her hands were fixated on ripping a sugar packet to shreds. "So…" She couldn't help but blush again. "This coffee, err hot chocolate meeting, is this something you would like to do more often?"

Inside Carly cringed, could she get any more pathetic? She just knew this was the part that he would say that this was just a one off thing and they would stick to their once a week PT. He took a sip of his coffee before he smiled, his light blue eyes sparkled back as he saw her blush.

"Listen Carly, I'm going to be blunt and honest with you."

Carly's heart plummeted and her stomach dropped, she dreaded his next words, she had heard them plenty of times in the past. To stop the hurt, she blurted out her own words before he could continue.

"It's ok, I understand Andy." Carly looked down at her

cup, her hands left the destroyed sugar packet and wrapped around the china and squeezed a little. Serves her right for getting her hopes up.

"Carly! Look at me." His voice was smooth, but held a hint of annoyance. "Baby show me those gorgeous eyes." Carly lifted her green eyes slowly to meet his own, he smiled, a small tilt of his lips.

"You don't understand, because you don't know what I was going to say." Carly wanted to speak but the stubborn look in his eyes made her close her mouth, she watch his hands reach over and engulf her own.

"How long have we known each other?"

Carly frowned as she looked at the tanned skin of his larger hand. "Fourteen months," she said quietly.

"Fourteen months," he repeated. "And do you trust me after all that time, after all we have talked about and shared?" Carly nodded her response.

"So trust me when I say this; I have wanted you since the day I met you Carly and it has been driving me fucking crazy holding myself back from you."

Carly blinked and just stared at Andy's face, she flicked her gaze to his eyes that showed only pure honesty as well as a hint of desire.

"Wha- what?"

"You heard me baby, I'm fed up of waiting. So yeah, to answer your question we will be doing this again and a hell of a lot more too, if I have my way."

Carly was stunned, he liked her. Words wouldn't form, so she just sat and stared.

"Carly," his voice lowered. "You have been mine since the night you walked into the gym, you just didn't know it." Andy stood and pulled on her hand. "Come and take a walk with me."

Carly collected her handbag from the floor and allowed Andy to lead her through the shop and to the exit. Thoughts raced in and out of her head. This was the kind of situation that she had only ever allowed herself to dream about.

"Wait Andy; stop for a second." She tugged on his hand as they neared the door.

"Why did you wait? Was I that horrendous to look at, was I that fat?" Carly tilted her chin and looked up into his face.

Andy frowned hard, she watched as his gaze travelled over her face. His own features turned almost angry. With no warning he pulled again on her hand, leading her out of the coffee shop, around the corner of the building and down the small alley that was there. Carly then found herself pinned between the brick wall and

Andy's hard body. She shivered as his hands travelled up her body, over the skin of her neck to cup her cheeks.

"Why did I wait? I waited until you were ready Carly. What kind of arsehole do you think I am that I would take advantage of you whilst you were dealing with your own shit?"

He shook his head then flicked his gaze from her lips, back up to her eyes. "You weren't ready then baby, but I don't think I can wait any longer."

His eyes blazed with need before he leaned forward and sealed his lips over her own. This wasn't just a simple kiss like in the gym, no this was a claiming and Carly wanted to be claimed.

Andy was in paradise, the taste of Carly's lips was intoxicating. The feel of her lush body pressed up against his own caused his blood to boil. His hands slid down her body and cupped her arse, a groan erupted from his mouth as her lips started a path down his jaw and neck.

"Fuck! Carly baby, we need to stop."

"Why Andy, I thought this was what you wanted?"

There was nothing sexier than the blush that travelled up her cheeks and the husky voice that said his name, it made his dick even harder at the thought that her whole body would be covered in that blush and he could quite soon have her moaning. She looked up into his face, her own looking slightly shy as she ran her tongue across her swollen lips. Her innocent question had him holding in another groan.

He took her face in to his hands and placed a quick kiss upon her lips. "Why?" he chuckled. "Baby girl, I want you so bad that my dick is about to rip through my jeans but I don't particularly want an audience."

He rubbed his thumb across her lips as he held her gaze. "I need you Carly. I have since day one. Come home with me…please?"

Andy waited for an answer, he loved how affected she had become even by just a kiss, she always seemed so shy but he didn't have any doubts that she would be a vixen once he got her home, home and naked. If she would have him. This may seem sudden to some but in his head, Andy counted all the times they had been together at the gym, all the times they had talked and laughed together.

He nearly missed her nod, but her sweet innocent smile managed to fire his blood even more. He grabbed her hand and almost dragged her from the wall of the coffee shop and down the street.

"Hurry Andy, I need you too," Carly admitted and he watched as she blushed once more, surprising herself with her admission.

"Fuck baby, that's exactly what I wanted to hear." He smiled as she giggled, her lips still so obviously swollen from his assault and her hair a little messed from where he had had her pinned. Carly squeezed his hand as they hurried along, her whispered words had him stumbling before he upped the pace.

* * *

Excitement thrummed through Carly's veins as Andy practically dragged her to his flat. Her feet barely touched the floor and she was unable to hold back a giggle when she had admitted to Andy that she needed him just as bad. He had moved like a man possessed and she loved it. She felt like their entire relationship had been leading to this point, every meeting, every touch. It was like the entire fourteen months had been a courtship of sorts and now was her chance to grab what she knew she wanted and not let go.

She wasn't just jumping into bed with any man. This was Andy, the man that she admitted had held her heart for a long time and now that she knew he felt the same, there was no holding back on her part.

Within moments they had arrived at the block of flats where he lived, he had them up the stairs and outside his front door in a matter of minutes. Andy unlocked the door but stilled, Carly placed her hand on his muscled back, concerned that maybe he wanted to change his mind already.

"Andy, are you ok?"

He nodded and pulled her hand up and around so he could and kiss her palm, his voice a little breathless. "Say no now Carly if you don't want to do this and I will wait, no matter how long it takes till you are ready."

Carly could see a muscle tick in his jaw, his body trembled a little and proved there and then that he fought against his overwhelming need for her. Carly had never had this, never had a man admit to wanting her so much as Andy did right now.

"Andy," her voice echoed in the passageway. "I want this, I want you." Carly again licked her lips and stepped closer towards his body, his muscles bunched in reaction to her touch on his arm.

"Andy. I'm yours."

Carly couldn't suppress the squeal that fell from her mouth as Andy quickly tugged her into his arms and meshed his lips with her own. One hand cupped the back of her neck and held her to him, he placed his free arm around and under her arse cheeks and lifted. Her legs eagerly wrapped about his waist, Carly groaned at the feel of being lifted and forced so close to this man that made her feel so much. He kicked open the front door and stalked into his flat the power of the kick sent the door rebounding off the wall and back into its frame, shutting it with a click. Their lips still sealed, Andy moved them down the hallway and straight into his bedroom.

Carly couldn't get enough of Andy, his taste was heaven and she actually whimpered as he pulled away from her lips and slid her body down his own. His eyes blazed with unconcealed lust and the physical evidence was pressed against her belly. Hot and hard, she couldn't help but gasp. His lips curled into a grin and he pulled her tight against him, chest to chest, pelvis to pelvis.

"Feel that baby girl, that's all for you."

His words, instead of shocking her, made Carly tremble with need as his hands made quick work of removing her jumper. She watched as Andy slowly slid to his knees in front of her, his gaze locked on hers as he pressed open mouthed kisses to her bare stomach. His fingers undid the buttons on her jeans before he slid them down her legs. Carly placed her hands upon his shoulders for balance as he pulled at her boots and freed her feet from the material.

Carly stood in only her underwear and she for once didn't feel self-conscious or undesirable, she was no virgin but her experience had been limited. This man made her feel beautiful, as well as sexy and gave her the confidence to take what she wanted. She watched as he stood in one slow, fluid movement, his eyes filled with heat as he pulled at his own clothes. Her eyes roamed over every muscle and banked each dip and valley to memory. His chiselled arms wrapped around her waist and once again pulled her tight against his own body. His mouth teased at the edge of her lips.

"I hope you are ready Carly; I plan to take my sweet time with you."

Carly nodded and gently pushed her fingers through his hair, still stunned she was in this room here and now about to have one of her dreams come true.

"What's that smile about, baby?" Andy said as he rubbed his palms up and down her upper thighs, sending tingles shooting through her body. Usually Carly would have answered with

"nothing", but Andy had a way of knowing when she was lying, so she told the truth.

"Just thinking how I'm about to have a dream come true."

Andy stood slowly, he reached for the hem on his t-shirt and lifted it up and off his body, Carly couldn't help the gasp that escaped her as she reached out to touch his chest with her fingertip. Andy remained still as she explored his body. Each muscle was clearly defined, showcasing his strength and making Carly almost giddy with delight. What turned her on more was when he flexed his biceps as he reached around her and tugged her into his body. For her, large biceps meant strength and strength meant protection.

Stupid and silly but that was what she had always thought.

"So, are you going to tell me what this dream is?"

Lifting her face to press a kiss to his lips she answered honestly, "My dream was to be with you Andy, like this." She grinned as she reached between them and finally cupped him, in turn bringing out a heavy groan that had her blood pulsing. Andy was hot and hard, and all hers.

"Baby," Andy groaned again

"Yes, Andy." She smiled and pressed her lips against his again.

"I wanted this to be slow and- God!" he croaked out as Carly moved her hand up and inside his now unbuttons jeans. "Fuck it," he groaned.

Releasing her grip on Andy's cock, Carly was pushed slightly away. Andy, his eyes never leaving her, kicked his jeans and boxers off. She had only a second to admire his naked form before he stalked back towards her and pushed her back against the wall, his breaths sawed in and out and his cock bobbed with each exhalation. He pressed her shoulder blades back against the cold wall before he let his hands travel down the length of her body, he stopped briefly at her hips and the continued downwards, taking her panties with him.

His harsh voice filled the room as he started back up, laying small kisses along her skin; thighs, then stomach before he reached her breasts.

"Do you know how long I have wanted to get you like this?"

Carly could only shake her head, she had forgotten how to talk as each touch Andy gave her sent flames into her bloodstream and stoked a fire she knew only he could quench.

"Since the moment I saw you," Andy admitted as he made quick work of her bra, gently cupping her breasts and teasing the nipples to hard aching peaks. Carly's chest heaved, her nipples had always been sensitive but she now felt like she would combust against the wall if something wasn't done.

"Andy…please."

He leaned in and pressed his lips to hers as he slid his hand back down her body and towards her core, his hand and fingers finding heated flesh that wept with pleasure at his invasion.

"At least now I know where you got waxed," Andy admitted with a groan. "Fuck baby, so wet," he continued as his fingers gained entrance and started a slow rhythm, his thumb pressing down on her tender, engorged clit causing a cry to fall from her lips.

"Fuck baby, I don't think I go slow, not now I've seen you like this, so hot and wet." Taking his hand from her core, he wrapped it around her thigh and brought it up to his hip, opening her up.

"You ready for this Carly, you ready for me?"

"Yes, yes," Carly panted as her own hands found his shoulders and she curled her leg around his waist.

"Please," she begged, and was rewarded with a brutal kiss. She felt his weight dip, then pressure at her entrance as he aligned the broad head of his cock. He rubbed it back and forth across her clit, making her tremble before he pushed. Carly felt needy, almost to the point of irritability, she lifted herself a little using his shoulders and moved her hips slightly, finally forcing the head of his cock to slip just inside her core, making them both groan.

"Carly, I wanted to try and go slow," he ground out, even as his hips flexed in and out in tiny increments.

"Fuck slow Andy. I need you…now!"

Carly cried out in pleasure as Andy once again meshed his lips with hers, at the same time he plunged inside her, seating himself to the balls.

"Oh God!" she cried out, her nails digging into the skin of his shoulders as he started a relentless pace that hit every nerve. Carly was in heaven, she had never felt like this before, she felt like her body was no longer her own.

"Fuck Carly, you feel so good." Andy's words were short, but said it all. On each inward stroke he hit just the right spot that would have her soon seeing stars if he just kept it up.

"Oh, oh just there…oh god, don't stop," Carly cried out.

"Hold on baby, we go together, ok?"

Carly nodded and buried her head in his neck as she held on for the ride, his thrusts becoming harder and deeper. He lifted her leg higher and ground into her, causing another cry to erupt from her lips. With talented fingers, he reached down with his free hand and pushed against her swollen clit, teasing and tweaking it until she teetered on the edge of the abyss. He leant in and whispered into her ear as he pinched the nub and slammed into her repeatedly

"Come for me baby, let me hear you scream my name."

Carly had no way to stop the orgasm that slammed into her as he played her body like an expert, her nails dug harder into the flesh of his shoulder and she bit down on his neck, her scream escaping, although muffled. His thrusts became erratic as Andy hit his peak, a groan leaving his own lips as he found his release, his hips slowing until they both sagged against the wall, their heavy breathing the only noise.

"Wow," Carly whispered.

"Wow," Andy answered.

CHAPTER THIRTEEN

Andy opened his eyes and grinned, he looked down at his chest and saw the spread of brown hair that lay splayed out as his Carly lay asleep. Her right hand was tucked up and under his ribs and the other clutched at his bicep, as if scared he would leave while she slept. There was zero chance of that happening; he would like nothing more than to stay like this for a long time.

With a tilt of his head he looked at his wrist watch, 5pm. They had only been asleep for the past hour, but the time spent before that had been the best time of his life. He doubted he would ever forget the feel of their bodies locked together, her nails biting into his skin or his name on her lips as he brought her to release over and over.

Andy used the arm that wasn't locked down by Carly's tight grip to sweep her hair away from her face, sleepy eyes met his own. "Hey, gorgeous." She blushed but smiled a sleepy smile before she rubbed her cheek affectionately against his chest.

"Hi," she answered. He grinned, there was nothing better

than seeing her blush, especially as it travelled from her chest and up towards her face.

"Want a drink, baby?" Reluctantly he let her sit up and away from his body, he wanted nothing more than to drag her back into his embrace, but he hadn't been a very good host so far and wanted to make sure she was looked after.

"Sure, water's good for me." Her voice carried a husky edge to it, one he hoped he had caused by making her scream numerous times.

Andy climbed out of bed and grabbed a pair of running shorts from the chair by the bed.

"Stay there baby, I will be right back, I'm not finished with you yet."

* * *

Carly's eyes followed Andy and watched his bare arse flex as he tugged up a pair of shorts, she had to bite her lip to stop herself from groaning out loud. The cocky grin he sent her proved he knew what had her all flustered. With a wink he left the room, leaving Carly to deal with a hot flush as she remembered what they had done a few hours before.

Unbelievably she had zero regrets about what had happened; it had felt right and she only hoped Andy felt the same and would like to repeat the experience.

Carly wedged the sheet under her arms and slid off the bed in search of her purse and in turn her phone. She checked that she hadn't missed anything important before she fired a quick text to Robyn.

To Tart @5:10pm

Carly couldn't stop smiling as she sat back on the bed, her life was now starting to fall into place. She already knew she had strong feelings for Andy. She wouldn't have fallen, well, jumped into his bed if she didn't. She was pulled from her inner musing by the doorbell, followed by Andy's voice as well as that of another.

Carly bent and collected one of Andy's discarded t-shirts from the floor and tugged it on, as well as her panties before she peeked out of the bedroom door. A stunning blond stood in the doorway, a pleading look upon her face as Andy scowled down at her. Now this was the sort of woman she had always imagined Andy to be with.

Unable to keep quiet, she edged out more.

"Andy, everything ok?"

She must have surprised them both as they both turned to look at her, the blonde's eyes widened before she smirked and a look she didn't recognise flashed across Andy's face before it was hidden.

"Yes, fine." Andy's tone was harsh. "Might be a good idea if you get dressed, I've got to go to the gym." His voice was cold and distant and his eyes never met hers as he turned to face the blonde once again.

Carly closed the bedroom door and quickly located her clothing. She dressed then retrieved her handbag and phone as she attempted to fight back the tears that threatened to spill. It didn't take a genius to realise that something was going on between those two. That, coupled with Andy's harsh words so soon after their afternoon tumble hurt more than Carly was ready to admit. Maybe it was best if she just left. Her logical side had said all along that he was well out of her league.

Fully dressed, she opened the bedroom door and walked towards the front door, both set of eyes watched as she drew closer.

One laced with sadness and the other a look of smug indifference.

"Carly, you don't have to leave." Andy looked down at Carly as she stood by the door. She lifted her chin and met his gaze head on, her voice calm.

"Yes, I do and it's probably for the best, I will leave you both to

it."

The blonde then moved so Carly could walk out of the door. Her face clearly showed she was enjoying the little drama.

"Carly, please."

"Don't Andy, I get it ok. I just…yeah, goodbye."

Carly turned and walked away, she bit into her lower lip to stop a sob from escaping. Yes they had only been 'together' for a few hours, but she had known him 14 months and had in all honesty fallen for him not long after they had met.

CHAPTER FOURTEEN

Carly's thoughts were in a whirl as she walked home, she didn't doubt that she looked a mess but she couldn't give a shit. Her phone vibrated from inside her bag, but she left it where it was, she really couldn't be bothered to check it right now. Why did she always have the worst luck with men? It just proved that no matter your weight, they all tended to be arseholes.

"Princess, you alright?"

Carly jumped in surprise and lifted her head to see Simon in front of her. She had just turned down the alley that was a shortcut to her house, but it also went past the back of the gym.

"Shit Simon, you scared me."

She went to move past him but he grabbed her elbow in a bruising grip.

"Carly, are you ok?" His words were softer than his grip.

"Yes, sorry Simon, I'm fine thank you, I just want to go home." Carly again tried to move past Simon but he refused to budge.

"Did you not like the gifts I sent you Carly? I made a

special effort with each one." his voice sounded strange, almost flustered.

"Gifts? What Gifts?"

Carly's stomach dropped, she had a good idea what he was talking about and she now wished she had mentioned it to someone, but she never thought it would be as serious as this.

Simon smiled again, but this time it was a cold smile.

"Yes gifts, the flowers and notes I left you after every session you did at the gym." Simon's grip became tighter and Carly tried to pry his hand away.

"Simon, get off me, you are hurting my arm, now let go." His gaze turned angry as she started to fight his hold.

"I make all that effort for you and you don't even acknowledge it, but you are happy to be with that prick, Andy. You are a cock tease, Carly. Not to worry, you will learn your place soon enough."

"What the fuck Simon, get off me!" He grinned and pulled a white cloth out of the back pocket of his jeans.

"Oh, you will learn princess." He tugged her closer and thrust the cloth into her face, over her nose and mouth, it gave her no choice but to inhale the fumes from the cloth.

Carly's vision started to dim as the effects of the chloroform took effect. Her body crumpled and she lost consciousness, unable to fight the pull to darkness.

* * *

Simon carried Carly's unconscious form into the back door of the gym, he made sure no one was around before he shut the door and turned to make his way down the corridor to the basement. Unused equipment was propped up against the wall and free weights had been dumped here and there.

He walked through another doorway and into the makeshift living quarters he had made for Carly. Ever since he had seen her six months earlier he had wanted her and had hoped that she had taken the hint and figured it out: that he was the one that was sending her the gifts and love notes.

He was desperate for her to notice and come to him, but she hadn't and instead seemed to tease him from a distance and make him jealous by flirting with that piss ant, Andy. It had taken months of planning and sneaking around, so Andy wouldn't notice and he was able to get things ready. But now he finally had her. He always got what he wanted and Carly was no exception. She would learn that he was all she would need and want, even if he had to persuade her. Simon stalked into the farthest room of the basement, one that had been left to disrepair and placed his new charge on the small camp bed. He would have to pop out again soon to get some more supplies as he hadn't expected to grab her so soon. He had been lucky though, today had been his practice run for seeing if the chloroform would evaporate from the cloth if he put it in his back pocket, he just never expected to get to use it properly on his intended. Simon didn't want Carly venturing out at all, so he wrapped both her wrists and ankles with duct tape. Carly would soon come to realise she was his, she had no choice.

CHAPTER FIFTEEN

Andy growled at Alexa. Why wouldn't she just take the hint and leave? It pissed him off that she had thought to look down on Carly like she had.

"Wow Andy, I thought you didn't date clients?" Alexa said. Her voice grated on his nerves.

"That's really none of your business Alexa, you've said what you needed to, now you can fuck off." He knew he was being harsh but he didn't care, this woman had fucked his life around once before and he would be fucked if he would let her do it again.

"Now that's not very nice Andy; you gone all moody and sour." Andy growled again.

"Well that happens when you are fucked about by a cheating slapper who bags anything with a dick." He paused and folded his hands across his bare chest, he had forgotten to put a shirt on but there was no way he was inviting Alexa in just so he could do that.

He continued on, "Oh wait, apparently you will screw anything without a dick too!"

Alexa looked furious and Andy felt a wave of satisfaction

as she stomped her foot before she huffed and walked off down the hall, shouting over her shoulder, "I won't be going back to your shitty gym

Andy, I can do better!"

Andy slammed the door shut and muttered, "Good riddance."

Seriously did she really think that he gave a rat's arse about her anymore? He had stopped that shit when she had trampled on his heart. But what really pissed him off was that he had lost his shit at Carly because Alexa had pissed him off with her attitude. He had wanted to talk to Carly, to tell her what was going on and how she had nothing to worry about. But he would be fucked if he was going to do that in front of Alexa, there was nothing he wanted less than her knowing his personal business. So he'd had no choice but to watch her leave, taking a piece of him with her. Dammit, if only she had stayed in bed, he could have got rid of Alexa and explained everything to her alone.

But fuck, the look of hurt on her face as she had left had hit him like a punch to the chest. He couldn't deny that Alexa's visit was an important one. She and a few of the other females from the gym had been having serious problems with Simon. One lady in particular was now at the gym waiting for Andy and the police to show up for a statement. Looked as though Simon had finally crossed that line and Andy couldn't wait to get rid of the prick. Andy needed to get changed and get down to the gym to sort this mess out, but he really needed to find Carly, she hadn't answered his calls or texts, she hadn't even read the texts, but he would keep calling. It ate at him that he had hurt her, he wanted to make things right, dammit.

He clenched his fists, if she had only stayed she would have seen there was fuck all going on between Alexa and him.

For fuck sake, didn't Carly realise that she was it for him? He had loved her since day one. Love is an intense word, and yes he was being soppy but he didn't care. He had waited long enough for his other half, so he would be fucked if he would let her go. Andy grabbed his keys and stormed out of his flat. A plan firm in his mind.

CHAPTER SIXTEEN

Carly felt hands on her face as she waited for the grogginess to subside. Her head felt like it was full of cotton wool and her mouth was drier than a nun's flip flop. Her mind was slow to process her current predicament; she remembered being at Andy's flat and then leaving and walking home.

As her hearing started to return, she heard words being spoken that at first were garbled, until her brain finally caught up and deciphered them. "Oh princess, I've always wondered if your skin was as soft as it looked, especially after watching you take those long showers."

Carly struggled to hold back a shudder as he continued to stoke her face and neck, she remembered now that it was Simon who had surprised her in the alley and used something to knock her out. Now she was laying tied up on a platform of some sort and he was spewing some shit about them meant to be together.

Carly opened her eyes and glared up at Simon whose own face was disturbingly close to hers.

"Ahh, awake at last," he sneered, his fingers continued to stroke her skin.

"Fuck you Simon, let me go!"

"Now now, that's a dirty little mouth you have there my precious, a lady should know her place."

His eyes seemed wild as they continued to roam up and down her body, his hand not touching her held a small carving knife and he seemed keen to wave it close to her face. Carly was petrified, her heart thundered in her chest and echoed in her ears, it took every ounce of bravery she had to face him without sounding as scared as she felt.

"How about you let me go you twisted fuck, before I scream."

Simon's face became distorted with anger and he grabbed a handful of her hair, she felt immense pain at the roots as he almost pulled it free. The knife pressed to her cheek, almost drawing blood. She cried out a little as he pulled her face closer to his own, his putrid breath nearly made her gag as it washed over her face before he slammed his lips on to hers, his teeth latched on to her lower lip and pulled a cry of pain from her. His voice was almost a growl when he released her lip and pulled away.

"You will have more respect for me now, Carly. I have you where no one will find you and you are mine."

He reached past her and grabbed a roll of duct tape, quickly pulling a piece free and forced it over Carly's lips.

"Now, you will behave and sit nice whilst I leave for a short while to go get you something more suitable to wear. I will let you have some food as well, but only if you are a good girl." He smirked and let his hand move up her thigh, until he pushed it against her core.

"And then, once I'm back we can get better acquainted; I have waited a long time to make you mine." He moved his hand back to her thigh and squeezed as he got to his feet, with one long perusal of her stretched out body he left, the slam of metal doors echoed through the room. Carly closed her eyes and tried not to panic, that would get her nowhere and she needed a way out of this, sooner rather than later.

Her wrists were tied together with duct tape, so tight that she had no movement, her ankles had been taped the same. Carly decided she would get out, there was no other option, she slid her body to the end of the bed and looked around the room, looking for any idea of where she was and if she could find a way free.

Her small bed was in the corner of the room, it was surprisingly comfy and large enough for two. That made her shudder again, Simon was proper tapped in the head if he thought she would let him touch her like that again, never mind use this bed for what he wanted. Turning over she looked around the room, her heart stuttering when she noticed a small bag left open on the floor. Inside she could see the bottle of chloroform that had been the key to her passing out earlier, but also two large serrated knives. Her gaze soon travelled past the bag and to a table that was just behind. The table was low enough that she could see it was full of random items but the wall behind she realised, was full of pictures. Pictures of her filled the space, ones that had been printed off from her Facebook page, ones that had been taken without her knowing, some dating back to when she had started at the gym. As she sat up taller she recognised the items on the table as being some of her clothing that she had convinced herself she had lost, but they had been stolen from her locker. In his sick and perverted way, Simon had created a sort of shrine dedicated to her, complete with pictures he must of taken when she had been in the shower. Her stomach rolled as she remembered all the messages, emails and notes she had received, along with the times she had been convinced someone was watching her, she should have taken it all seriously, but then again, does anyone actually think it will happen to them?

"Fuck," she mumbled, hating the feel of the tape on her lips. Carly shook her head, now was not the time for what ifs, she had to find some way of getting out.

CHAPTER SEVENTEEN

She still hadn't answered any of his calls or his text messages, even her best friend had only received one text and that had been before she had left his flat. Andy was now sat in his office at the gym, his phone in his hand as he continued to call Carly. He had also yet to get a statement from the lady attacked by Simon, to make sure she was happy that the police had been informed and she would give them a statement. He needed to be careful with how he dealt with this.   The police being involved just showed how serious the event had been. Andy was pissed at himself that he had missed the signs, this could cause a lot of bad press for the gym.

"Andy, are you busy?"

Andy's head snapped up and he smiled and lifted his hand to motion a clearly shaken Sonja into his office.

"Come on in honey and take a seat."

Nearly two hours later, Sonja had left and the police had taken over his consult room and were now taking statements from other clients that had issues with Simon. He was surprised that they were all females and were all ready to press some kind of charge against him. Andy had what he needed now to sack the sick bastard, but he doubted he would get a chance seeing as the police were keen to arrest him. He was a goner, pure and simple, but what made Andy really nervous was being told of Simon's continued obsession with Carly. He had been heard numerous times making lewd comments about her.

Andy tried her mobile again and cursed when it wasn't answered, he slammed the mobile onto the counter before he turned back to his paperwork. From speaking to Carly's best friend, he knew that she had tried to get hold of Carly as well, but with no luck. Now he had to type up the report from his perspective, it needed to be done, but all he could focus on was Carly, he would keep trying her mobile until the police were done, then he would go and find her. Out of the corner of his eye he spotted movement on one of the cameras that fed the live footage from the CCTV placed around the gym. It clearly showed the image of the back of the gym, where the door was located that went into the basement. He watched as Simon's form dived through the door, his arms burdened with bags.

"What the fuck?" Andy mumbled to himself as he stood. He called out to one of the trainers that were sat on the reception desk to send the police to the back straight away, he had a feeling all of their questions would be answered soon. Andy knew he should probably wait for the police, but something in his gut told him he had to go and now. He pocketed his phone and made his way quickly out of the front of the gym and round to the back.

* * *

Carly's hands were free. It had taken a few attempts, but she had finally pulled off that trick that she had seen on Youtube of how to get out of having her hands tied by duct tape. She had quickly untied her ankles and removed the tape from her mouth. All that was left was to see if her handbag had been left nearby so she could find her phone and then get the hell out of here.

The sound of metal doors caused Carly to frantically search for a place to hide, or at least for something to use as a weapon. Her eyes landed on a loose 5kg weight that had been wedged under the camp bed. Carly was quiet as she slid it out and moved towards the back of the door, the weight held up in her hand ready to slam into that piece of shit's head.

"Oh princess, I hope you have been a good girl, have you…where the-" His voice was so slimy that it literally made her skin crawl, so she had no qualms as she lifted up the weight and brought it down hard on his head as he passed through the doorway. As the weight connected, it made a loud crack followed by his cry of pain as he hit the floor, his bags scattered. Carly immediately dropped the weight and tried to bolt out of the door. Before she had got a foot away, Simon reached out and grabbed her ankle, tripping her up and bringing her to the floor with him, instantly he was on her, trying to subdue her as she bucked and scratched. "Get off me!" she screamed as she raked her nails down his face, she was desperate to get away.

"Fucking bitch!" Simon shouted as he grabbed one of her wrists and tried to stop her attack. "You will pay for that and for all the times you teased me." She fought back the bile that shot up her throat as he wedged a thigh between her own legs and pressed into her, ripping a cry from her.

"NO!! Never." Blindly she reached out, her hand falling on the dropped 5kg weight, she lifted it and aimed it at Simon's head once more, smashing it into the back of his skull. The sounds of metal on flesh filled the room, followed by the slump of Simon's body over her own. Carly felt herself start to hyperventilate as she pushed him off her, blood pooling around his head from where she had hit him, but she didn't care. As soon as she was free she once again bolted for the exit, her arms pumped hard as she ran at full pelt. Her eyes scanned for a way out, so frantic she never saw Andy stepping into her path until she had barged into him.

"Carly, oh fuck baby are you alright?"

Andy had somehow managed to stand his ground as Carly had ploughed into him. As soon as he had wrapped his arms around her waist she had at first panicked until she had realised who held her.

All she could do was sob into his shoulder as she crawled up his body, wrapping her legs around his waist.

"Baby it's ok, I've got you." He cupped her face in his hands and looked into her tearful eyes. "Where is he?"

Carly looked up and nodded towards the corridor she had bolted out of, echoes of pain filled groans confirmed Carly's answer.

"Andy Jackson?" A voice called out from behind, Carly clutched at Andy's shoulders harder.

"Yes, thank you for following."

"Thank you for your help, we are done with the interviews, all we need now is Simon O'Connor's location."

Carly watched Andy as he spoke to the police, both seeming to understand exactly what was going on and were in the process of dealing with it.

"Yes, Simon is down that corridor, by the sounds of it he's suffered a slight injury, nothing he didn't deserve though, I'm sure."

Andy turned and started to walk towards the exit with Carly in his arms.

"Please don't worry, we will take care of everything from here, if she is not injured we will need a statement, so please wait for us inside."

Carly watched as Andy nodded, then tucked her head into his shoulder as he walked out into the night air.

CHAPTER EIGHTEEN

UNDAY 13*TH* FEBRUARY - 10:30PM

Andy looked down at the sleeping form of Carly all tucked up in her bed, the events had been too much and she had passed out as soon as the police had left. His saving grace was that she had clung to him throughout the visit and hadn't gone to sleep unless he was holding her hand.

He wanted Carly to wake up so he could tell her exactly how he felt. Simon kidnapping her had cemented for him how he felt about her and he hoped that she would forgive him for being a complete arse.

"Andy?"

"Hey baby girl, how you feeling?" His hand clutched at hers, he refused to let go and break that connection.

"Groggy and achy, but ok I guess. You didn't need to stay."

"Carly baby, I wanted to." Andy watched as she refused to meet his eyes. "Baby you know there is nothing going on with me and

Alexa right?" Her eyes flicked up to his, bingo he had her attention now.

"She came to me to tell me about Simon and she also pissed me off with her bullshit. I'm sorry I made you feel like I didn't want you there, that couldn't be further from the truth."

"So what is the truth then Andy? Because that fucking hurt."

Andy winced then tugged on her hand, he wanted her in his arms. "Come here."

Reluctantly she sat up and moved close enough so he could wrap her in his arms, he rested his chin on top of her head and let it out.

"The truth, ok baby, the truth is: you are it for me." She stiffened in his arms, but didn't move away.

"Ah fuck."

"Andy, what?" She tilted her head to look up at him.

"Carly baby, I fucking love you ok, I always have. It drove me crazy when I couldn't get hold of you and the thought of that bastard's hands on you makes me want to rip him a new one." Andy looked down as Carly's eyes filled with tears.

"Talk to me baby, please." Andy's heart thumped against his chest wall, he was certain she could hear it.

"You love me?"

"Yes baby, so much it hurts."

"That's good." All Andy could do was nod. Yes it was good, so fucking good he was about to panic because she hadn't said what he was so desperate to hear.

"That's good, because I love you too Andy."

Her answer had barely left her mouth before he meshed his lips with hers, branding them and her as his own and erasing the memory of Simon's foul touch.

"Carly?" he asked between kisses.

"Yeah Andy?"

"Tomorrow's the 14th February, will you be my valentine, for now and always?"

Her answering smile caused his heart to expand with joy.

"I thought I already was."

Their lips met again, this time at a slower pace, each touch laced with love and emotion, each breath from the heart.

A True Exercise in Love

EPILOGUE

1 *YEAR LATER, 14TH FEBRUARY*

Carly collected the last box from the back of the hire van and hoisted it up into her arms, she shut the door using her arse and then headed up the small path that lead to the blue front door of a small, three bedroom, semi-detached house. Blowing a wayward strand of hair from her face, she used her foot to knock on the door.

"Carly baby, I told you to let me get that." Andy mock scolded as he took the box from her, easily lifting the heavy weight into his arms and led the way into the house, down the hall and into the sparsely furnished living room. Only a few boxes and a used sofa filled it but it wouldn't take long to organise it and make it a home. Wiping her hands on her jeans she moved to look out of the window and out into the back garden, ideas of what to do with it in the winter filled her head along with the reality of what they had done.

Wow, Carly thought. She turned and watched Andy's muscled back as he moved the boxes then walked over and wrapped her arms around his waist from behind. She couldn't help but rub her cheek against the muscles of his solid back as she felt his hands grab hers, his thumb caressing her skin as he pressed them against him. *Wow*, she repeated in her head. Over two years ago, she would have never believed or dreamed that she would be where she was now; five stone lighter, a career she now loved and was proud of and a boyfriend that she adored. She was still convinced that he was well out of her league.

"You ok, baby?"

Carly nodded against Andy's back, squeezed him a little and mumbled, "Yeah, I'm good."

She knew her voice wasn't very convincing and wasn't at all surprised when Andy tightened the hold on her hands, lifted his arm and turned so she was now in front of him. He moved them to the wall beside the window, where he pushed her against it. Carly tilted her head to look up into Andy's blue eyes, easily ensnared in their depths.

"You going to tell me what's going on in that head of yours?" Andy grinned and bent his head to Carly's ear. "Or do I need to use my special art of persuasion?" He kissed the skin just behind her ear, making her shiver in response, before he asked again.

"What's wrong baby?"

The bastard, Carly thought. He knew full well her brain went to complete mush when he did this, his whole 'pin and distract' always worked to get him what he wanted and this time he wanted answers. Thing was, Carly didn't really want to give them. She didn't want him to know how petrified she was of losing him, she had seen for herself how many stunningly beautiful and skinny girls attended his gym and how many of them looked at him with open interest. Since she had met Andy, she had overcome so many of her issues and slain a lot of her inner demons but this, this was harder to get rid of and ignore. Andy had quickly become her rock when she needed someone to rely on and quickly after that, he had taken her heart too, becoming the man she felt she could turn to even though she still saw herself as not worthy.

"Carly?" Andy pushed.

"Nothing," she mumbled once again, and felt Andy's body tense, that had been the wrong answer. Since that first time they had been together, Andy had shown her plenty of things and opened her eyes as well, she had also soon found out that Andy had a slight dominant side, which she admitted she loved and revelled when he used his strength to show her how he felt. She found she loved the feeling of being pinned against a wall because he couldn't wait. But now, now she was nervous, nervous because she couldn't lie to Andy, but she didn't want him to see how deep her insecurities actually went. She felt his hands slide down her body towards her hands, before he had her wrists quickly pinned up and over her head, her breasts thrust out hitting his chest.

"That was not the answer I was looking for baby and you know it." Carly closed her eyes instead of staring back at his intense gaze, the feelings he instilled sometimes were just too great. She knew he would be smirking in that annoyingly dominant way he did when he had her in this position, but never once did she feel threatened. She could feel her heart pound against her chest, as it always did when Andy put his hands on her, but now she was afraid it would stutter and stop because it couldn't keep up.

"I-" Carly stuttered, heat flooding her face as she admitted, "I'm scared."

When Carly opened her eyes after the admission, she found Andy frowning down at her as he moved his hands down from her wrists and cupped her face, his thumb moving over her cheeks in a light sweep of skin on skin. "Scared of what, baby?"

She loved that he went from dominant to protective in an instant. Bending, he kissed her nose in a sweet gesture that spoke of the love he felt. Carly had moved her hands down to his biceps and she gently squeezed them before she answered.

"Scared that this," she looked around them, then placed the palm of her hand over Andy's heart, "and you will vanish like it never happened, stupid I know." Carly released a sigh. "I don't think I could cope if this was just a dream and I woke up and I was back where I started."

Carly was looking back out of the window as she said this and wasn't surprised when Andy forced her gaze back to his own, what did surprise her was the depth of emotion she saw mirrored in his own eyes.

"Carly." He said her name quietly, reverently. Goose-bumps appeared on her skin, as they always did when Andy's voice lowered in tone.

"This isn't a dream baby, I promise you, but if it was rest assured I would make sure I found you and made it a reality." He continued to stroke her cheek. "Everything you have worked so hard for baby, is real, it isn't going anywhere."

Andy bent his head again and kissed her lips, this time a brief connection of lips, but Carly felt it down to her very soul.

"But?" she questioned, there was always a 'but'.

"You forget baby, I can read you like a bloody book." He grinned and Carly blushed with embarrassment. Was she that easy to figure out?

"I know you think things through far too much and right now, in your head, you are convinced that I am going to bugger off with," he paused, "with a skinny bimbo...am I correct?"

Carly's eyes widened as he hit the nail on the head.

"Wha-? How did you..." she whispered, convinced he could read her bloody mind.

"I know things," he said smugly, before Carly narrowed her eyes and replied, "Robyn told you, didn't she?"

Instead of answering, he stepped away from the wall and

grabbed her hand, tugging her to follow him to the lone sofa. After he pushed some bags out of the way, he sat down and tugged her down on his lap so she sat sideways, his arms tight around her waist.

Robyn had met Andy officially not long after that event a year ago and thankfully after the expected threat of "If you hurt her, I will hunt you down and remove your balls with a rusty penknife", both Robyn and Andy had become fast friends and allies when it came to ganging up on her. She didn't mind at all, it just meant her family was getting bigger and she loved it. Andy's voiced pulled her back from the memories taking over.

"Carly, I love you," he said, his voice low once more. "I loved you since that night you first walked into my gym." Carly blushed more, what was it about this man that rendered her useless with his words?

"There isn't another woman on this planet that could pull me away baby, I told you a year ago you were it for me and I meant it."

He laughed as Carly buried her head against his chest in an effort to hide the fact her face had gone bright, tomato red.

"Do you honestly think I would have sold my flat and then bought this house with you if I didn't see us having a future together?"

Carly finally found her voice and lifted her head. "No Andy, you wouldn't have."

"Exactly," he answered. He leaned forward and kissed her forehead, the gesture was sweet and made her feel foolish for her doubts, but she couldn't help it. Thing was, she knew she would get through it because Andy was always so damn patient with her.

"I love you, Andy."

"I know baby," he answered, and then gently set her on

the sofa next to him. He took her hand, lifted it to his lips and kissed her knuckles.

"You are my world Carly, it's as simple as that." Carly couldn't help but smile, she adored the fact Andy was so open with regards to his feelings towards her, it made up for the fact she was the opposite and totally shit at revealing hers.

"Carly?" His voice once again pulled her attention from her own thoughts and to him.

"Yeah, Andy," she said with a smile as she realised that her hands had moved to Andy's large biceps and were slowly stroking them. His biceps had to be her most favoured part on Andy, she loved watching him do arm day at the gym and would always lose focus whenever he flexed his guns. But most of all, she loved how she felt when he wrapped those big arms around her, encasing her in his strength.

"Well for starters, you had best quit the molesting baby, unless you want our new neighbours to see what I like to do to your hot, naked body." Carly's hand stilled, but she felt her body respond at his words, she flicked her gaze to meet his.

He grinned wide. "I've got a pressie for you."

Carly laughed. "Is it a Freddo?" she asked as she leaned over his lap, patting his pockets in an effort to find the prize.

"Left pocket baby and watch where you're throwing that elbow, my schlong aint invincible you know."

His laugh filled the room, followed by Carly's lighter one as she searched in his left pocket until she found the slight bulge.

"AHA," she called out as she reached inside his pocket and pulled out the really small velvet drawstring bag, only about two inches squared in size, obviously not a Freddo, Carly pouted.

"Don't pout baby, I've already put your stash of Freddos in the fridge, this is something different." Andy pulled Carly back against his body, his arms around her waist and his chin resting upon her shoulder. Carly just held the bag in her hand, confused on what it might be.

"Go on baby, open it."

She tipped the contents of the small bag into her right palm, she felt Andy's breath deepen on her neck as she looked at the item that now lay in her hand. There, shining in the sunlight lay a ring of white gold, the ring itself textured and showed it had been handmade, but what took Carly's breath away were the stones that dominated the ring itself, the centre stone was about 8mm round and was a stunning, un-polished ruby. The red so deep it reminded Carly of her mum's dark red lipstick she used to wear. Either side was flanked by two 4mm unpolished quartz stones. Even though they were unpolished, they still glistened in the sun and each facet shimmered, mesmerising Carly.

"Andy, this is beautiful," she whispered as she tilted it from side to side.

"You like it?" Andy asked as his hands left her waist to take the ring from her fingers.

"It's amazing Andy, stunning," she answered honestly, her eyes followed the gem ring as he took it from her, her eyes so entranced she missed his question.

"I'm sorry, what?" She turned her gaze from the ring and looked into Andy's eyes, surprised to see a hint of worry in the usually shining blues.

"I said," Andy repeated, "Tomorrow's Valentines Day baby, would you be my valentine?"

Carly recognised the words as the same ones he had spoken a year ago, she couldn't help but interrupt him as he spoke, she already knew the answer to this question.

"I already am Andy, you know that."

"Let me finish woman!" He chuckled before he grabbed her left hand and slid the ring onto her third finger, the fit was perfect.

"Carly, would you be my valentine for now and always,

would you be my wife?" Carly's eyes widened as she looked from the ring on her finger to the face of Andy, almost like watching a tennis match she continued to do this until Andy stopped her.

"Carly! Look at me."

As requested, her gaze met his own as he said the words even more clearly.

"Carly. Will You Marry Me?"

Stunned and dumbfounded, Carly could only stare, her heart thundered in her chest and she was convinced he could hear it. She couldn't answer, not yet, and as if he knew she was unable to talk, he continued on.

"Baby, let me love you for the rest of our lives, be the only one that gets to annoy you for always."

He paused and reached up to wipe a stray tear that unknown to Carly, had escaped and ran freely down her cheek.

"Don't cry baby, I just want to make you happy for the rest of your life." He smiled and leaned forward to kiss her lips again, his voice a whisper. "Will you let me Carly?"

Carly smiled and felt her world shift once more, twenty eight months ago she had made the choice to change her life for the better and now, Carly could safely say she had done just that.

Her voice just as quiet as his, she breathed the words before she sealed her mouth over his and let him feel all the love she felt.

"Yes, Andy. I will."

ABOUT THE AUTHOR

J. Thompson is a USA Today Bestselling Author of Paranormal and Sci-Fi romance and a major fan of procrastination. Jenn has always loved history, so using her wild imagination and tying in her love of history and fantasy, she began a new adventure into the world of words. Weaving romance into old worlds and giving life to her mythical inspired novels is what Jenn does best, and she has a lot more planned in the future, including some hard assed demons. When she isn't bent over her laptop with the crazy writer eyes, you will find Jenn making jewellery, cross stitching and it doing paper crafts. Jenn is also an avid lover old skool skills like archery and sword fighting.

Maybe a touch nuts Jenn is an author who believes wholeheartedly that people are good and that everyone deserves romance - even Hades.

Connect with Jenn online at:
Soulmatenovels.com

Keep up to date with Jenns Newsletter
Here